His

Boyfriend's

Rookie

A Contested Possession Novel

Sasha Avice

ISBN EBOOK: 978-0-6452714-6-1

ISBN PRINT: 978-1-7635380-0-9

Cover by: ashwood designs

Edited by: Copy by Kath

Newsletter

Subscribe to my newsletter via sashaavice.com for regular updates on WIPs, new releases, and thoughts on writing.

You'll receive two free novellas upon sign up.

Just want the books? No dramas: hit unsubscribe after you've downloaded them.

This one's for Ana...

1

♥

J OQ LAUGHED AGAINST THE guy's lips, felt the answering
smile in the clack of teeth as they kissed. He pushed his hips
forward and felt the guy gasp. Joq grinned. The guy huffed.

"Yeah, okay," the guy said around his panting breaths.

"Okay?" Joq asked as he pulled out, waited, and thrust back in.

"Ah, fuck," the guy squirmed where Joq had him pinned to the
mattress with his dick buried to the hilt, his hands holding the
guy's in a firm grip over his head.

"Good?"

"You know it is," the guy panted.

And well, yeah. Joq did. He slid all the way out, watched the
guy suck in a breath and brace for it, and pushed back in hard.
He found a rhythm and let the guy's hands go so he could better
bracket himself over him, his forearms on either side of the pillow
so they could kiss properly.

His phone rang. Joq paused.

"Really?" the guy asked.

Joq leaned over to the bedside table. The new angle nudged the guy
awkwardly, and Joq felt his grunt rumble through his abdomen. The

screen lit up with George's name and the frowning picture Joq used for his contact.

It was from a holiday in the Greek islands in the off season several summers ago. Joq had woken George up by rubbing up against him with excessive enthusiasm to get him to laugh. George had frowned, chuckled, shoved him away and Joq got the picture. George's dark hair was a mess against the white sheets, his serious brown eyes slits as his face got stuck between a frown and a smile. It was one of Joq's favourite pictures. George had asked him repeatedly not to use it: 'In case someone sees.' Joq shook his head every time George said that. George never looked at Joq when he asked, and Joq never looked back when he replied, 'No one's gonna see.'

The phone stopped ringing and the screen went black. Joq would call him back. He brought himself back over the guy.

"You sure you don't need to get that?" the guy asked. "'Cos, I mean, I can just wait."

Joq grinned. "If I picked up," he drew his hips out so just the tip was inside, watched the little uptick of the pulse in the guy's throat, the sweat trickling over it, "I wouldn't stop," he shoved back in.

"Ah, fuck," the guy's back arched as he bared down on Joq's dick. "You like talking to your mum while you fuck random dudes?"

Joq laughed and started fucking the guy for real.

After he made the guy come, got himself off a few thrusts later, he pulled out and the guy hissed.

"Sorry, sorry," he said as he rolled to the edge of the bed and removed the condom.

"All good," the guy panted.

Joq stood, picked up his phone and hit the missed call.

George picked up after a few rings.

"Hey," he said.

"Hey, thought you'd be in the air by now?" Joq replied and looked at his reflection in the floor to ceiling windows, the blinking lights of the city beyond the hotel room.

"Delayed."

Joq was still panting. He sucked in a deep breath, ran a hand through his short blonde hair, dark with the sweat. "You wanna talk—

"Sorry, you're busy," George cut him off.

Joq huffed a laugh. He looked over his shoulder at the guy in the bed, met his sleepy eyes and shared a smile.

"Nah, just a hook up."

"Any good?" George asked.

"You know I don't kiss and tell," Joq winked and the guy chuckled, rolled over with a groan.

George snorted. "Since when?"

"Since I'm still lookin' at the guy's ass." He watched the guy's body shake with a laugh, his face buried in the pillow.

"I'll let you go then," George said.

"I'm kidding. What's up?"

"Nothin', just delayed."

"Hmmm," Joq went for the mini-bar. "You're nervous."

"I'll talk to you when I get back."

Joq got out a beer, slammed the fridge shut. "He doesn't know who I'm talking to."

"Joq, don't."

Joq cracked the beer open and took a swig. The guy rolled over and raised an eyebrow.

"Fine, I'll talk in code. You meet him yet?"

He could hear George breathing down the line. Joq knew he'd either end the call or take the offer.

"Tomorrow," George said after a while. "I don't envy him."

Joq shrugged and drank his beer. "You been through it, he'll be fine."

"Yeah," George sighed. Joq knew he wanted to talk about it. George's own entry to the league as the most promising rookie of all time had gone well, obviously, but it hadn't been easy; the pressure, the expectations, the terror that he'd fuck it up before every game. When Joq met him that first season, George had been a scared eighteen-year-old kid hyperventilating in the locker room after everyone else had gone home for the day. Joq was new himself, but there was a pretty big difference between working security in the surveillance room as a twenty-one-year-old uni grad who couldn't find anything better and playing to hundreds of thousands of opinionated, asshole fans.

"Babe, come on, it's different now—

"It's worse," George said, clipped.

Before Joq could reply, George cut him off. "We're boarding. I'll see you at home."

He hung up before Joq could reply. Joq shook his head and tossed his phone on the bed.

"Boyfriend?"

"Yeah," Joq said and got back on the bed, rested his head against the headboard. The guy sat up and took the beer from his hand.

"You gotta go?" he asked after he had a swig.

Joq took the beer back and sipped. "I got time."

"Nice," the guy said and Joq smiled down at him.

He finished the beer and decided to make good use of that time. This guy was a lot of fun, easy, when things with him and George had been anything but lately, if ever. Joq finished the beer and rolled over so he was over the guy again.

"Hi," the guy said.

Joq quirked his lips and kissed him instead of answering.

2

H E KNEW THEY WERE coming down the tunnel before he saw them, the sound of so many voices Joq couldn't make out any individual words. It was accompanied by the kind of amped laughter that meant the press conference was done and had gone well. Joq rounded the corner and saw George smiling broadly, his head slanted to look at the rookie beside him, the Great Finnegan Flynn.

Joq had seen pictures, obviously; they didn't do the kid justice. He was gorgeous. Young and awkward too, but it was already evident he would grow into a striking man. His eyes were fixed on George, his smile blinding yet endearingly shy in the way of a kid meeting his idol.

Joq kept his line and approached. These situations were always tricky: George would either nod an acknowledgement and keep going or stop and say hi, indulging in the narrative of him and the security guy that'd been best friends since George's rookie year. 'Joq's too,' he'd end with, and whoever was around would laugh in that way that said: isn't George a good guy, making friends with this regular dude.

Joq was almost on top of them by the time George looked his way.

"Joq," he said, surprised, his smile settling to the normal one. Everyone else kept moving—assistant coaches, PR people, the CEO and management team—but George stopped and Finnegan stayed close by his side.

"George," Joq said and suppressed his smile. He could feel the rookie looking between them, could almost feel the sunshine vibes he cast off. Joq remembered reading something about the kid coming from Byron Bay, and he swore it radiated out of him like the calm buzz of someone grown in a pot of marijuana, anti-vaccination rhetoric and home schooling.

Joq turned to him as George spoke. "This is Joaquin, Joq, runs surveillance in the stadium."

"And you must be the great Finnegan Flynn," he said and extended his hand.

The kid huffed. "It's Finn," he took Joq's hand in a firm grip, quite the contrast to the way his eyes were flitting from George's to Joq's to his dress shoes.

"Your parents called you Finn Flynn?" Joq asked as he pumped his hand.

"Yeah, they're assholes," he replied and took his hand back. His smile didn't dim as he tilted his head down, let the golden curls and sun-bleached strands fall in his face as he blinked big eyes up at Joq, his mouth twisted in a playful grimace.

Joq laughed.

Goddamn. Kid was cute. And definitely gay.

That was a surprise.

Joq felt his dick take interest; he imagined Finn had that effect on a lot of gay guys. Probably straight ones too. Shame he was too young.

George cleared his throat. "We better keep moving."

Joq looked at him and raised an eyebrow.

"Yeah, yeah, course," Finn said. "Nice to meet you, Joq. See you round?"

Joq turned back to him. "You'll find me lurking in the shadows, yeah."

Finn giggled, an incongruous sound for a six foot kid who wouldn't have been out of place as a Michelangelo carving. Joq couldn't help his answering smile.

"Alright," George said and placed a hand on the kid's back as he got them moving. "Time to face the team. Later, Joq."

"George," Joq said to their backs. "See you later."

He watched them head down the tunnel, George's hand lingering on the kid's suit jacket as he said something too low for Joq to make out. They made a nice picture in their perfectly tailored suits, the fabric stretching over concealed muscles. Joq always did like an athlete in a suit. They disappeared into the locker room and Joq headed for the surveillance room.

He had his own team to see and a new person starting, the niece of an old friend. She'd dropped out of uni and stated flatly in the interview: 'I don't give a shit about football, I just need the fucking money,' to which Joq had replied, 'You're hired.' She had the skills of course, but Joq liked that in her; she reminded him of himself.

He decided to focus on where to slot her into the roster rather than the twinge of something unsettling in that meeting. Of course George was going to be protective of the kid—that wasn't news, Joq had watched him working himself up over it for months. Ever since they got the confirmation Finnegan Flynn, number one draft pick from two years ago, was ready to join the team after his stint in the state league following some injury that had prevented him from joining at eighteen, George had been talking about it. Combine that with starting as Head Coach and all those assholes in the media waxing poetic about how he was 'too young, he should do his time as an assistant first' and George was worked up. Well, as much as George got worked up—said less than usual and exercised more—but for George, that was damn near hysterical. He'd ask him about it when they got home tonight.

"Alison," he said now as he pushed into their break room just outside the surveillance room.

She stood, her lips stretching into a line that passed as a smile. "Joaquin."

"Call me Joq. Come on," he went for the surveillance room door. "Let's get on with it."

He caught her smile widening as he opened the door. "What?"

She shook her head. "Nothing, just. I fucking hate small talk too."

Joq grinned. "I knew I liked you." They went in and he introduced her to Cameron and Simo and ran through the monitors.

"Wow," she breathed out when he was done.

He turned his head and raised an eyebrow at her.

"I mean," she waved her hand. "You can see everything."

"Kinda the point," Simo said and bit into a liquorice strap.

"No, I mean, I get that, but," she pointed at the monitor on the top left corner. "The showers?"

"That gonna be a problem?" Cameron asked and winked at her.

She laughed. "I'm gay."

"Nice," Simo replied and nodded, chewed, looked her up and down. Joq could practically see the lesbian fantasies from straight porn playing out in his head.

"I meant more, isn't that a privacy violation?"

"Not if it's for protection," Joq said. "And we're not watching the players shower. Here, look," he leaned forward and hit a button to change the camera. The entrance and exit came into view, obscuring the view of the locker room showers. "This is the view we use. We just have that one if needed. If something happens."

Alison nodded and looked through the monitors. "It's pretty extensive."

"Every inch, baby," Simo said and took a swig from his Red Bull. "Here, look."

Joq crossed his arms over his chest and watched as Simo showed her that they did, in fact, have a view of every inch of the place. During games, they brought up the stadium views and the surveillance team split between monitoring the private areas, the player areas, the offices in the top of the building, and the crowd areas. The security on the ground had mics connecting them to the team in this room. Game days were all hands on deck.

"Does anything ever happen?" Alison asked.

"Not really," Joq said.

"Hey now, we caught that racist that time," Cameron said.

Joq felt his phone buzz in his pocket as he listened to Cameron regale Alison with the story of how they helped management locate a fan who'd racially vilified an Aboriginal player.

"Got her banned for life," Simo finished.

Joq looked at his phone.

Gonna be a late one. Don't wait.

Joq frowned.

I'm gonna be late too. Text me when you're done.

He watched the screen for a while. No reply. He pocketed his phone.

"Come on," he said to Alison. "I'll show you around in person, show you what we're looking at."

"Make sure you smile up at the cameras," Simo winked up at her.

She snorted.

"We'll be watching, baby," Simo went on.

"Simo, you're one comment away from a sexual harassment charge," Joq said.

Simo laughed.

"Don't worry, boss," Alison said. "I don't feel harassed."

"Thanks, baby," Simo said.

"I feel pity," she said around a smile.

"Burn," Cameron snickered.

Joq held the door open and let her go out first while he watched Simo laughing, rocking from side to side in his chair. Joq rolled his eyes at him and followed her out, the door sucking shut behind them.

"This way," he said as they left the break room. He took her through the stadium, pointed out the cameras at each point, and she was a good sport about it—waving, giving the finger—and Joq imagined the glee radiating off Simo. It didn't take much.

As they headed through the second tier, Joq saw the press conference playing on the screens they had up so people getting food wouldn't miss anything during a game. He stopped. Alison was a few steps ahead before she turned back and came up alongside him.

"I think he's gonna surprise you all. He's certainly better than me, got a better head for this sh-... stuff as well..." George was saying, his hands clasped on the table, microphones in his face, a little smile at the almost slip up.

The shot flicked to Finn laughing beside him, holding nothing back, his blue eyes dancing as he looked at George.

The camera panned out to a shot of the two of them. George was hunched forward with his head craning back to meet Finn's gaze. Joq watched closely as they exchanged a look and a smile that acknowledged they were in this together, a budding camaraderie.

"*Yes, about you,*" a reporter asked. Joq knew him as one of the guys from the talking heads footy shows. "*There's been a lot of talk about whether or not you're ready for this. Care to comment?*"

"Asshole," Joq said. "He was born ready."

"Fan?" Alison asked.

George was answering the question with the prepared response he'd been practicing on Joq since they gave him the job: he understands and appreciates the reservations; he understands this is an honour and a privilege; he loves this team and has no plans to blow this opportunity... blah, blah, bullshit.

"Sort of," Joq replied. He glanced at her. She was watching the screen. Doing a pretty good job of feigning interest. "George and I started here at the same time. We're friends."

"Really?" she glanced at him.

"Really," he looked back at the screen. "He's a good guy, he doesn't deserve to be undermined like this before he's even started."

"Huh."

"What?"

"Just friends?"

Joq looked at her. She was watching him back.

"I know you're gay, Aunty Kat said. Sorry, maybe she shouldn't have... Just, you sound kinda protective of him" she shrugged.

"You signed an NDA too." Joq heard himself blurt that out and wondered at his sudden burst of defensiveness.

She rolled her eyes. "I don't need a non-disclosure agreement to know not to be an asshole. Anyway, it's none of my business."

The thing was, outside of Joq's circle of very close friends, his immediate family, George's sister and parents—albeit reluctantly—he and George were firmly in the closet as a couple. There was speculation about George because of an old rumour, but no one in this world knew about them officially.

He had a disorientating moment as he realised this was the first time someone had asked.

"I'm gay," he confirmed. "But we're just friends."

"Ah, I get it."

"Get what?"

"Crushing on your straight friends," she nodded sympathetically.

He looked at her. She was smiling at him like she was happy to follow his lead. He cracked a smile; he could play it off like, yeah, what can you do? But something about the way she was looking at him told him she suspected there was more to it. He trusted her aunt—she'd been his neighbour back in his Brunswick share house days—and Alison gave off the same solid vibe.

Joq started walking again. "Just, don't tell another soul, alright? He's really private."

Her little heels were loud on the concrete, the building cool around them.

"I don't even really know who he is," she replied. "And I don't care. But yeah, obviously I'm not gonna say anything."

"He's George Creed," he said as he swiped his security card at the door that'd take them upstairs. "And if you work here for more than a week, believe me, you're gonna know who he is."

3

♥

JOQ WAS STANDING NEAR his car in the empty parking lot when George came out of the building. It was dark and there was a fine mist of rain, which was strange for December, but a welcome relief from the heat.

"You didn't have to wait," George said as he strolled over.

Joq clicked the immobiliser. "Just finished myself. I told you."

George grunted an acknowledgement and got in the passenger's side.

The headlights lit up the droplets of rain as they headed out, the soft sound of Joq's trance CD filling the space between them. He refused to put the radio on in the car. He didn't want to hear the shit on there about George, and he hated the way George pretended it didn't bother him, then went and brooded about it for days afterwards.

"Thanks," George said after they'd been driving for a while.

Joq shrugged. "Might as well when we can."

George grunted again, shuffled around in his seat, and gazed out the window. Their schedules rarely coincided during the season. But even if they did, sharing lifts every now and then as 'buddies' was unre-markable, coming and going together every day might raise questions George didn't want to answer. Joq had always found it extraordinary that nothing about their 'friendship' had raised a single eyebrow. Everyone seemed happy to eagerly buy the friends-who-lived-nearby bullshit they'd spun for a decade.

"I saw your press conference," Joq said.

He expected George to groan or huff, brush it off like usual. George didn't, he stilled. It was the kind of stillness only someone who knew him as well as Joq did would pick up on.

"Yeah?" George asked eventually.

"Not all of it." Joq glanced at him.

George was watching him back.

"What?" Joq asked.

George shook his head. "Nothin', just the usual bullshit."

That response was not nothing. George liked to talk about the bullshit. He liked to plan his offense; he hated being on defence. Joq was going to watch it as soon as he got a moment to himself.

"So, Finn seems alright," Joq said as he pulled up at their gate. Well, technically, it was George's gate, George's place, but Joq had been living here for ten years, moving in after they'd dated for two. He felt entitled to call it their home.

George grunted and didn't elaborate. Now, that was suspicious.

"What?" Joq clicked the button for the gate and they waited for it to open. "You seemed to like him."

"Course I like him, he's on the team."

Joq turned to look at him. George was looking out the window. Joq cracked up. George whipped his head back. He was frowning, but he was trying not to smile as well.

"Oh my God," Joq said. "Old man's got a crush!"

George shook his head. "Can you just park the car?"

"You do," Joq whistled but did as he was told. "Pity he's too young. And he's one of your players. Oh and you never fuck around."

"Yeah," George said as he unclipped his seatbelt and got out.

Joq shook his head. George leaned back in and his smile was cheeky; it made him look young, look the way he did when they were practically kids getting together.

"More's the pity," he said and leaned over the console to kiss Joq as the gates slid shut behind them.

Later that night when George fucked him, Joq felt an edge to it, a desire bordering on aggressive. George had him on his hands and knees, his dick like steel as he pushed inside.

Joq groaned and arched his back, prepared for a pause to adjust but George was pulling out and shoving in, then again, fast and so deep it stole Joq's breath. He gasped as much at the fucking as the noises George was making—guttural breaths in tandem with his hips as he slammed into Joq so hard he slipped onto his elbows. George tightened his grip on his hips and pounded him harder. Joq got a hand on himself and jerked off furiously.

"Yeah, get yourself off, baby," George rasped.

Joq moaned and came. George never talked in bed. Never. And he rarely kept going after Joq came. He did now. It was almost too much—the way he was yanking Joq back onto his dick, like he couldn't help himself, like it felt too good to stop. Joq groaned at the thought as he felt George start to come.

George hadn't fucked him like that in a long time, like he was so turned on he'd finally turned down the noise. Nothing perfunctory about it. It felt good, it felt amazing, and as George pulled out, rolled over and promptly passed out, Joq thought this little crush might work out quite nicely for his sex life.

I T WAS STILL DARK when he cracked his eyes open the next morning to the sound of George moving around the room.

He groaned. George snorted. Joq felt the bed move as a hand planted itself near his hip.

"Go back to sleep," George whispered.

"Where you goin'?"

"Training," George kissed the top of his head.

"Hmmm," Joq grabbed him by the collar before he could pull away.

George huffed but met his kiss. It didn't hold the passion of the night before, the lingering effects of which had Joq wanting to drag George back into bed to do it all again. This kiss—quick with a hint of tongue at Joq's insistence before George pulled away—told him that wasn't happening.

"Bit early," Joq said as he rolled onto his back.

He heard George pause in the doorway. "Beach," he replied. "Go back to sleep."

Then he was gone.

Joq remembered the interview and woke right up as he reached for his phone. If George had broadcast his crush to the whole football watching world, Joq wanted to see it so he could give him shit for it later.

04:03 blinked up at him when he swiped his phone. That was early. Since when did beach training start at four in the morning? Even if it was still preseason, then six in the morning, okay, but four?

Maybe George was bringing in some military tactics. Joq had seen him reading books on discipline according to an ex-marine, and they'd chatted about the possibility of employing that kind of mentality. Joq recalled seeing military people training in the dark hours of the morning in a movie.

He sat up and found the press conference with a quick search. It opened with George and Finn at a long table, microphones in front of them, the team logo emblazoned on everything around them. They looked sharp in their suits, which Joq knew looked even better in person. George was sitting forward, hands clasped, his posture straight and commanding, his face calm if a little blank—standard. Finn was sitting back, his smile easy, his hair an absolute mess—surely someone was going to do something about that soon—and his lazy gaze kept drifting to George as questions were asked. Finn answered in his shy yet friendly drawl, while George gave his more typical clipped remarks, the odd smirk.

Joq yawned. There was nothing in this. For anyone who didn't know George, they'd think he was the tough, cool, calm player he'd always been. Only now, he was bringing that commanding presence to coaching. Or, he was going to try—and arguably fail—according to the media.

"*So you two just met this week?*" a reporter asked.

"*In person, yeah,*" Finn replied, looking at George who was leaning back to meet his eyes. "*But we've been facetiming for a while now, texting, that kind of thing.*"

George was nodding. "*Yeah,*" he said, eyes on Finn before he looked back out at the scrum, the cameras, "*I reached out after the draft, then again after he got the call up and we kept in touch. Thought I could offer a few pointers.*"

Finn's arm moved and George broke into a grin, flashed it at Finn before looking back at everyone else in the room. Joq realised Finn had just given him a playful tap on the thigh under the table.

"*A few pointers, he says,*" Finn sat up, chuckling. "*Think he was more worried about all this than me.*"

"*Hey now, it's a lot of pressure and I didn't hear you complaining when you called at midnight with every panicked thought a man can have.*"

"*That was one time!*" Finn laughed.

"*Anyway,*" George cleared his throat and schooled his expression. "*It's been good to finally meet in person, see what I'm dealing with.*"

Joq saw Finn's arm move again as they looked at each other and smiled.

The questions moved on to how George was planning to use Finn in the mid-field. Joq was gripping his phone. He loosened it. George never told him that. Joq had noticed he'd been on his phone more, but he figured it'd been the team in general, the new job. Surely all those calls in his home office, those texts at dinner, and yeah, those late night calls, surely they weren't all Finn?

Joq watched until it rolled into an advertisement, his mind drifting. Even if they were, so what? Joq knew George had been anxious about what Finn was facing, argued it was different now with social media. "Especially since these damn rookies insist on broadcasting their whole lives with that shit," he'd said.

Joq googled Finn. The first image that came up before the accounts was... well. It was an eyeful. Finn was standing on the beach laughing at someone off camera, his boardshorts loose on his hips, his abs the star of the shot. Joq swallowed. Washboard abs, lean yet cut. Joq clicked through more photos, then scrolled through various accounts, noticed the thousands of comments, and wondered what in the hell Finn's messages must be like.

There was a young woman in a lot of the pictures. Similar age, very similar looks—messy blonde hair, stoner blue eyes, straight white teeth; she was barely covered in a series of bikinis, tiny tops and shorts next to Finn's numerous shirtless pics, barely there singlets, their bodies comparatively perfect. Joq realised it was his sister when he saw their beaming faces alongside an older woman, another clone, looking up at the camera over a birthday cake. Finn's mum. Joq read the post and deduced she was a single mum, raised her two kids running her own, Joq groaned, naturopath and homeopath clinic in Byron. The rest of it was more of the same—beaches, lots of skin, bonfires, smiling faces, lots of guys around but no one in particular, so just a big friendship group and then the usual training, football highlight stuff. The follower numbers were staggering.

He checked out a few articles and pieced together what he already knew in a vague way. Finn was drafted two years ago. Then he got injured—developed osteitis pubis, a degenerative groin injury, and stayed in Byron to work with the best specialist for it, who happened to live there. Joq thought about the pictures with the sister, the mum, and wondered how true that was. Regardless, he'd worked his way back in playing in the local Byron league. Joq's suspicions about him being a mama's boy seemed confirmed when he read Finn played a year in reserves for match fitness in the NEAFL. Sydney and Brisbane turf. Why would a Victorian rookie play for the Sharks on the Gold Coast? Sure, he got experience against AFL listed players and wouldn't play against his team mates in that league, but it'd make more sense to come down to their reserve team.

What had George said in that press conference? '*Reached out after the draft, then again when he got the call up.*' The call up was three months ago. So, George had known the kid, in a friendly way, for over two years? And George had initially reached out when he was still a player. Then '*kept in touch*' for the last three months as his coach.

Joq got up and went downstairs. He clicked on the espresso machine and looked out at the pool. The lights were on, the whole tropical scene with the cabana and palms lit up against the dark. Joq shook his head, it was rookie-coach shit, nothing more.

Not much in the press conference to tease George about either, and it's not like Joq could ask him about the budding friendship that'd clearly been going on for months, years, without sounding like he was *asking something about it*. Which was ludicrous, George wasn't going to fuck the kid. Finn hadn't even turned twenty-one yet. A decade between them was like a lifetime to someone like George—he was way too far in the closet for that. Not to mention, George was nothing if not a total professional—he'd never risk team dynamics for a fuck. Never.

Joq shook his head and made his coffee. He watched the palms sway in the breeze, listened to the filter bubbling in the pool and decided to do some laps before he went into work.

But as he swam, he couldn't shake the thought of George talking to Finn, knowing Finn, for over two years and never mentioning it. It's not like he and George lived in each other's pockets, but something about this felt deliberate.

He sank back under the water, pushed his feet against the wall and swam to the other end. Maybe George didn't say anything because it wasn't worth mentioning. It was nothing. Joq came up and sucked in a pull of air. That was actually the more likely scenario—George said nothing because there was nothing to say. Finn was just another player, and now another rookie.

5

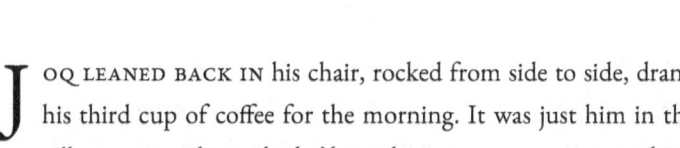

J OQ LEANED BACK IN his chair, rocked from side to side, drank his third cup of coffee for the morning. It was just him in the surveillance room this early; he'd get the team on a more punishing schedule once the season started, let them sleep in when all that was happening was training.

He leaned back and watched the security monitors in front of him. The wall of individual black and white screens captured the familiar tunnels and corridors, locker rooms, treatment rooms, the gym—the bowels of the stadium that'd been his daily view for almost twelve years.

George appeared on the top corner monitor. It still gave Joq a thrill. Not in the way it did in the early years of their relationship; there were no more butterflies or bolts of desire. It was fondness now. A comfortable knowing there was his man. It always made him smile.

George was walking down the tunnel with his assistant coach, his dark hair so long it brushed the top of his collar. Joq reminded himself to tell George he needed a haircut before the season started. The assistant coach was speaking, his hands waving, and George frowned as he listened. But then he looked up, his gaze landing on someone coming from the other end of the tunnel and his expression softened.

Joq glanced at the screen below and saw the back of Finn.

George said something to the assistant and walked on ahead alone, his face transforming into a smile like it was out of his control, a lightness in it Joq had never seen.

He glanced at the middle monitor as the two met in the corridor. Finn must've said something because George laughed, surprised and pleased. Finn looked down, his footy boot kicking at nothing on the concrete.

George said something and bumped Finn's shoulder. Finn glanced up and Joq took in the scene they made together—same height, but that's where the similarities ended. George was a man whose career as a player had come and gone and at almost thirty-one, he was the youngest coach to take the mantle. It showed. He had gravitas, but he had the nerves of a first day at the office too. It made him seem younger.

Next to Finn though, he was indisputably a man. George filled out his open collar white button-up, his dress pants, and suit jacket with the impressive physique of a man who'd used that body and used it well. He had laugh lines around his eyes. They crinkled while he looked at Finn now. Finn—every inch the super star on the cusp of twenty-one in his shorts and practice jersey against his unblemished tan skin. The way his head dropped down in a desire to please, in an attempt to hide his shy smile; it was nothing like the confident kid in those social media posts.

Joq had watched George live his life on these monitors with players and coaches and trainers for years. He'd never seen anything like this. He was sure he was imagining it, layering his own filthy fantasies over the scene. He couldn't help it—he knew George wouldn't go for it, but he'd had a few idle daydreams. Few men wouldn't in the face of Finn. And George crushing on Finn. He imagined being asked to join them. A frivolous thought: George was not a man to do threesomes. It was still amazing he was with Joq at all. But watching them now, those fantasies spoiled in the way only a previously unwavering infatuation with someone can spoil when they do one innocuous thing—the wrong cologne, a rude remark to a waiter, an uncensored look.

He watched as George reached out, casually brushed Finn's wrist, his thumb stroking the skin in a few quick sweeps as he spoke. Finn's expression smoothed to serious. He nodded his head in a sharp jerk before his face broke into a smile. George dropped his hand, said something close to Finn's ear and then moved on. Joq watched as Finn turned, laughing, his eyes fixed on George's back.

Joq flicked his eyes back to the top monitor and watched as George shoved his hands in his pockets, smiled to himself and walked down the corridor. It was nothing, banter, team stuff—

And then George looked back over his shoulder and Joq couldn't see his face, but he glanced back at the centre monitor and saw the way Finn blushed, his smile shrinking to self-conscious.

Joq leaned back in his chair, clasped his hands over his abs. Surely George wasn't going to finally take advantage of being in an open relationship by hooking up with the rookie... was he?

6

♥

THE THING WAS, THERE'D been a rumour. Joq didn't hear it until after he'd met George, after they'd slept together in Joq's cramped room in Brunswick. He'd only just started at the stadium, and as the newest guy on the roster he got the odd weekend off. Sitting in a bar around the corner from his place, he'd been drinking a beer, watching the game, watching George and feeling flushed and tingly seeing him up there on the screen when he heard it.

"Ya know he sucks dick?" a guy on the other side of the bar said to his friend. Not loudly, just part of their regular conversation.

"Get ya hand off it," the friend replied and shoved him lightly.

"It's true! I read about it."

Joq paused with the beer to his lips.

"Oh well, it must be true then. If you read about it," the guy's friend gestured to the bartender for another beer.

"Nah, man, it was on like, one of those threads. And I know like, that's usually bullshit or whatever, but this was like, the other dude's sister's friend that said it," he waved at the screen where George was lining up for a shot on goal. George pulled up a bit of grass, threw it in the air to assess the wind, then fixed his eyes on the goal posts from the awkward angle.

He kicked. The crowd in the bar hushed. A rippling of sound started up as they watched the ball follow the intended line and scrape through for a goal.

"Fuckin' beauty!" the guy's friend yelled. Everyone was clapping, cheering. "If he can kick like that, he can suck all the dick he wants!"

Joq watched George on screen getting mobbed by teammates, his face so young he had the look of a man who hadn't fully shed the boy yet. His smile was small, which would become the norm for him; a quiet joy which radiated beneath the downcast eyes, the closed mouth smile. He always looked like he was barely containing his happiness, and yet he had no idea how to express it, if it was even okay to express it.

The guys in the bar didn't bring up the rumour again. Joq finished his beer and left before the game was even at half-time.

He remembered trawling through a lot of bullshit on the internet before he found it.

It was more than a blowjob. The author of the post claimed he'd heard about it from his friend, who knew the sister of the guy George was with. And that was the story: he was with this guy in high school. Everyone in the town kind of knew it, and everyone kind of dismissed it. George was going to the AFL, George was the only claim to fame this little Victorian town would ever have; everything else was irrelevant.

It was a nothing story on a dark corner of the internet. Joq was curious about the guy. George never brought up another guy. But George kissed and sucked and fucked like he knew what he was doing. He was eighteen years old, and he was no gay virgin. It actually made sense when Joq thought about it beyond his excitement at fucking around with a guy as hot and chill as George.

But at twenty-one, Joq was yet to develop the courage to confront a man—even the young version—as impenetrable as George.

It was a year before it came up. The dark recesses of the internet found their way into a more mainstream gay blog; an article speculating on closeted, gay athletes. Nothing hit official channels, but it was hard to miss the chatter. Even harder to miss how closed off George was, how twitchy; twitchier than usual when it came to arranging their dates and hook-ups. And Joq would've been a fool to miss the timing of George disappearing on him for a month.

Busy was the clipped reply when Joq messaged. Then George stopped answering his calls. He stopped dropping by. Joq almost ignored him back when George finally did message asking to catch-up.

They'd fucked, quick and frantic with pent up energy, and after, lying naked and sweaty in Joq's bed, he'd finally asked.

"Is it true?"

George exhaled roughly on top of his already laboured breathing. He sat up.

Joq rolled onto his stomach and looked up at him. George was young but he looked tired then, hunted. He met Joq's eyes then skittered his gaze away, jerked his chin, eyes on the wall.

"Are you gonna confront him?"

That got George's attention; he looked at Joq, his forehead creased. "Who? Alistair?"

"Yeah? I mean, is that the guy?"

George rubbed his face. "He didn't do anything wrong."

"He outed you without your permission."

But George was shaking his head. "He didn't. His sister knew about us, we..." he peered at Joq, then glanced away like a boy recounting a crime, "used to, you know, at their house after training."

"Was he your boyfriend?"

George shrugged, picked at nothing on the bedspread. "Yes and no," he ran his hand over the material and watched the path he made.

"Yes," he said after a while, firm. "He's apologised. And Tammy, his sister, is horrified it got out like this, some girl in the salon must've said something... But like I said to him, it's nothing. It'll blow over if I ignore it."

Joq sat up and pushed himself so he was sitting next to George against the headboard.

"You could come out?" he said tentatively, his eyes on George's hand. He remembered the way George had frozen.

"I'm never gonna come out."

"But—

"No, never. Look," he placed his hand over Joq's; his skin had still been smooth, his brown eyes wide, innocent, "I like you, I like this, but if you're wanting that, I can't ... I'll never do that."

"What about when you retire?" Joq had asked the question expecting an affirmative answer. He'd already imagined it, expected it.

It'd felt so surprising at the time when George said, "Never," so vehemently Joq had no idea how to reply.

"I really like you," George went on, lacing their fingers together, "but I get it if this is not gonna be enough for you."

Joq shook his head. "We'll make it work."

"Yeah?" and George had sounded so grateful, all Joq could say, with the certainty of a twenty-one-year-old, was: "Definitely."

He often wondered if he negotiated being open shortly after because he wanted something of his own or he'd hoped to provoke George's jealousy. Probably a bit of both, depending on the day.

He never met Alistair, was never invited to George's home town, but George mentioned him casually, fondly, whenever he came back from visiting his parents—"Saw Tammy, she says Alistair's good, got a good job in the States."

"Cool," Joq would reply—what else was there to say? Joq got the feeling these country town people gossiped about and protected their own in equal measure. That whole aspect of George's life was closed to him.

He saw a photo once—a tawny eyed, tawny haired young guy in a flannelette shirt and work pants, work boots, George next to him in the same get-up. Both boys wore understated smiles as reluctant eyes met the camera, their reverie with a thermos of coffee and sandwiches on the floor of a shearing shed broken by the intrusion.

"Who's this?" Joq had asked when he came across it buried in George's desk drawer.

George had looked over his shoulder. "Alistair," his voice had been gruff yet warm. He'd busied himself with making space on the bookshelf for Joq in his home office but Joq remembered the feel of the guy in the room with them, like George's memory was a private, fond thing and simply saying the guy's name brought it to life. Joq looked at the photo and imagined them finishing up for the day, making excuses to go back to Alistair's place, closing the bedroom door and exploring each other wordlessly, breathlessly, their inexperience made up for by a mutual, unspoken desire.

But the point for now was, while George had managed to stay firmly in the closet, and kept his relationship with Joq in there with him, it was out there. Floating around in the football world as idle gossip, mentioned and dismissed, but very much known to anyone with ears. Finn had ears. And Joq would bet his annual salary Finn had heard the rumour and was one of the few who hadn't simply dismissed it.

7

♥

T HE SMELL OF A roast permeated the kitchen as Joq made a salad, heard George come in the front door.

"Hey," George said around a smile as he entered the kitchen and came over to Joq, his hand going around his waist as he kissed his temple.

"Hey, dinner be ready in ten," Joq replied.

"Nice," George nodded at the salad before he turned, whacked the top of the door frame, went back down the hall and upstairs to get changed.

Joq had a plan. Invite the rookie over for dinner. Probably start calling him by his actual name rather than 'the rookie' or 'the kid' in his head all the time as well. He didn't know why he was so fixated on that, but it wasn't really important.

He needed to focus: if George and Finn were such good friends then George should tell Finn he was in a relationship with a man. Finn was clearly gay, it'd be good for him to know he wasn't alone. And it wouldn't be the first time—Jack Reaver—ex-team mate, friend, also gay—knew about them. He'd guessed, and Joq confirmed it, which had pissed George off no end, but Joq had argued, rightly he thought, "What's the harm? He's gay too."

So, why not Finn? It made sense for Finn to meet Joq more formally, to be taken into the wider family so to speak. Finn was away from home, young, it made sense to offer him a broader support network. A 'safe space'—Joq imagined a kid like Finn would be into safe spaces.

Joq had the outside table near the pool set when George came out again.

"This looks good," George said as he took a seat.

Joq rolled his eyes. "It's chicken and salad, babe. I make it all the time."

"Still," George smiled at him. "It's what you do with it."

Joq laughed at the joke. It was a line from a movie and they ran it whenever Joq cooked.

They settled into a comfortable silence and ate, enjoyed the breeze, the soft tunes wafting from Joq's speaker. Joq waited until they were finished and he was sipping on a beer, George drinking his soda water, before he broached the subject.

"So, I saw the press conference."

George took a deliberate sip of his water, swallowed. "Yeah?"

"Months, huh?"

George shrugged. "It's true what I said, thought he could use the support."

"Hey, I think it's cool of you, but I was thinking..."

George looked at him and waited. He was calm, but those handsome features—the serious eyes, strong jawline, classic profile—were chiselled by time and transformed to guarded more readily with each year.

"You were thinking?"

"We should have Finn over for dinner," Joq swigged his beer.

"Why?" George sounded scandalised, like Joq had suggested they have Finn over for a threeway.

Joq raised his eyebrows.

"He should know we're together."

"What? Why should he know that?" George stood.

Joq looked up at him. "Because he's gay and you're friends?"

"He's not," George shook himself before he could finish the lie. "He doesn't need to know about us. Why would I tell him that?"

George cleared the plates and went inside.

Joq watched him through the windows. He waited. *Why wouldn't you tell him?* He wanted to yell. But he wasn't much of a yeller, and anger got him nowhere with George. He cleared his throat, tapped his fingers on the table.

George came back out, beer in hand. Joq hid his surprise.

"You should tell him," Joq said.

George glanced at him. "I don't see why."

"You said it yourself, he needs the support. If he saw this," Joq waved his hand with the beer between them, "he'd see what was possible."

George sighed, took a drink of his beer and looked at the pool. Joq waited.

"I'll think about it," George said after a while.

"Yeah?" Joq smiled up at him.

George huffed, but returned the smile, small and quick. He knew Joq wanted more, wanted more people to know, still wanted to be open one day. Joq had told him he got it, but telling another person was an olive branch—a way for George to concede more ground on keeping them so secret.

That's what Joq told himself this was. And he knew that's what George would see this as. Joq didn't think too much about the part of him that knew that wasn't all this was.

A COUPLE OF WEEKS later, George came home from training and said, "Friday."

Joq raised both eyebrows. "Friday?"

"Yeah," George breathed out. "We'll be here at seven."

"We?"

"We might as well come home together, after training," George said defensively.

"Makes sense," Joq nodded.

George let out a long breath. "Yeah."

Then he went upstairs and Joq ignored the flutter of nerves in his stomach.

9

♥

IT WAS CLOSER TO seven thirty when Joq heard the front door open, the sound of unfamiliar laughter beside George's deep voice.

Joq took a deep breath, exhaled and turned as he felt them come into the open plan kitchen-dining-living area.

"Hey, babe," Joq said. It sounded awkward. He didn't understand why he said it.

Finn was smiling at him but it faltered. George looked affronted and surprised.

"Hey," George said. "You remember Finn."

Joq screwed his face up. "Uh, yeah," he rolled his eyes and went forward to shake Finn's hand.

Finn smiled, returned the handshake politely as George said, "And you remember Joq, from surveillance."

Joq felt that like a slap. "Bit more than that," he grinned. It felt strained.

An odd silence followed. Joq waited for George to fill it. He didn't. Finn took his hand back and looked around. Joq saw the blush radiating up from his clavicles, moving up his throat and heating his face under the tan.

"This is nice," he said.

"Like you haven't got nicer in Byron," George tapped him on the ass as he went for the fridge. "You want a beer? Joq gets the low cal stuff," George smiled at Joq.

Right, Joq knew this George. This was George putting on a good publicity display and shoving all other feelings down. He could do it in the face of the most outrageous media questions, he could do it at strained family dinners with his Catholic family, and apparently, he could do it when his boyfriend accidentally outs him when he thought that's what they were supposed to be doing here.

Joq smiled back. George maintained the media smile before turning to Finn's laughter.

He took the beer George handed him and clinked their bottles together. "True, Byron's pretty nice, eh? But this is still pretty sweet."

Joq watched them as they stood together at the open door, admiring the pool, the garden, the cabana. They were both freshly showered, damp hair curling at their collars, and while George had changed back into his team training gear, Finn was dressed in a nice polo shirt and tailored shorts, like he'd brought the clothes with him especially for the dinner.

"I've never been to Byron," George said.

Finn bumped his shoulder. "You'll have to come visit. It's actually the best, I'm just tryin' to be nice."

George laughed and bumped him back. Joq stood there, eyes fixed on their backs as they got into a playful hip checking match, traded joking insults, and laughed together.

"BBQ," Joq said, too loudly.

George and Finn startled and looked back at him.

"I've got to cook the BBQ," Joq said.

"Hey, no, I can do that," George said and came into the kitchen. "Finn can help, try and get some meat in his hippy ass."

Joq's eyebrows went up. George grinned at him as he took the meat tray, and Joq felt like he was smiling back, while Finn laughed. Right, just the usual homophobic jibes these guys used as the glue to build a team dynamic.

The salads were already made, so Joq busied himself with taking them out, getting the plates and utensils, and every time he went out he listened and stole glances at the pair at the BBQ. He didn't think he'd seen George smile this much, laugh this much, in years. It was clear he had an easy rapport with the kid, which should've made Joq pleased for him—having his super star rookie in hand would make his life much easier. If only that's all this was. And Joq couldn't figure out if it wasn't, but something in the little shoves, the quiet smiles, the gazes held a moment too long made every nerve stand to attention on Joq's body.

By the time they brought the cooked BBQ over, Joq had polished off half the bottle of wine. He expected George to give him shit for it, but he didn't even seem to notice. He was giving Finn a friendly bump in the direction of the seat to his left at the head of the table, and then sitting and beaming at Joq to his right.

"Looks good," George said, genuine and pleased like he was commenting on more than the dinner.

"Looks the same as it always does," Joq poured himself another glass of wine.

"Then that's a sweet set-up," Finn said as he took the salad bowl George handed him. "BBQ by the pool every night, home cooked food."

"What're you eating? Take-out?" George asked him.

"Mainly, yeah, but I been getting those boxes too with the recipe and all the shit. My mum set it up," Finn replied.

Joq held his plate up when George handed him a piece of grilled steak.

"You can cook?" Joq decided to get his shit together and join the conversation. He nodded his thanks at George and looked at Finn.

Finn was blushing again at Joq addressing him directly and Joq had no idea why. Sure, Joq knew he was easy on the eyes himself, and he'd been pretty open about being gay and being with George, but he was very much an acquired taste with his fine, Nordic features, his lean build. And besides, based on everything he'd witnessed so far, the crush here between George and Finn was reciprocal.

"I can follow a recipe," Finn smiled, bashful.

"Very open to instruction," George agreed, nodding.

Joq rolled his eyes. "Alright, well this is not a training drill. It's family dinner, so eat."

He did not miss the way George shot him a look for that, nor the way Finn hid his face in his hair.

Joq had a big drink of his wine. "Oh, come on," he started and looked between them. Then he turned to Finn. "You know we're together right? We're trusting you with that."

"Joq," George said, his knife clattering to his plate.

Joq ignored him, kept his eyes on Finn. Finn glanced up, his eyes were on Joq but his attention was all on George.

"I know that now," he said and glanced at George as if for permission. Then he looked back to Joq. "You know I'm gay."

"Yeah, I figured that out," Joq said. "I'm not trying to out you. Sorry," he shook his head. "I'm trying, very badly, to say it's okay and we're here if you ever need us."

"So, you're like," he looked down at his plate and swallowed. He looked back up, glanced between them. "Really together?"

"Yep, twelve years," Joq said.

"Oh," Finn looked back down. "That's cool."

"It is," Joq said and looked to George for help. He didn't get why this was going so badly.

George shook his head at him, but before he could say anything, Finn spoke again.

"Must be nice, having someone."

Joq watched as he sipped his beer and looked between them before his eyes landed on George.

"I've accepted that I'm basically never gonna get laid again until I retire."

Joq almost choked on his mouthful. Finn was giving George a cheeky grin, then turning a dialled down version onto Joq.

George was shaking his head. "Well, it's not like I get as much dick as this one," he nudged Joq playfully.

Finn looked confused.

"Oh, shut up," Joq finished his wine. He decided not to dignify that with a response.

He was taken aback when George did.

"We have an open relationship," George said to Finn. "We can't be out "'cos, you know. So," he shrugged and cut into his steak before looking up, straight at Finn, "it's a compromise."

"Oh," Finn said, his face red. He was smiling as he studied his food, and replied softly, "Cool," head nodding as he repeated, "Cool, cool."

Joq looked at George. George shrugged as if to say, *isn't this what you wanted*?

And Joq wasn't sure this was what he'd wanted at all.

It was late by the time Finn left, George waiting with him for an Uber out the front. It seemed like a lot of time had passed before he came back in.

"That went well," he beamed at Joq once he was back in the kitchen.

Joq sipped on the beer he'd cracked after he'd finished stacking the dishwasher. He needed it.

"Yeah," he said and picked at the label, tried to pick out his words carefully.

"Finn liked you," George said and went to the fridge, got himself a bottle of water.

"I think he liked you more," Joq replied. And well, so much for choosing his words carefully. Sue him, he was drunk.

"What's that supposed to mean?"

"I think you know," Joq levelled George with a look. Surely he wasn't going to play dumb.

"No," George said slowly. "What I know is he's a rookie with a bit of idol worship. But don't worry, he's getting to know me. He'll be over it soon." He laughed and came over to where Joq was sitting on the bench. "You comin' to bed?"

Joq shook his head and looked down. He didn't know whether or not to push it.

"Yeah, just, I know we're open—

"Oh, I know you know we're open," George squeezed his hip and moved away.

"But surely you're not thinking..."

George paused in the doorway, his back to Joq. Joq knew he took his meaning.

"I'm thinking we're in an open relationship," George said firmly and walked out.

Joq took a deep breath and exhaled slowly. He didn't know how to say to George that if he fucked that kid there's no way it'd just be a fuck. If he said that, he'd be admitting... what? Something he wasn't even willing to admit to himself.

He shook his head and finished his beer. He got another one and went into the living room, clicked on the TV.

As he sat and watched the late news, he told himself twelve years wasn't nothing. And if George finally wanted to take advantage of their arrangement, then that was his prerogative. It's not like Finn—hot, outgoing, and endearingly shy in the way only someone so young could be—would be looking to settle down. It seemed the best course of action was for Joq to play it cool and let it play out. Be there when George came back.

10

♥

T HE SEASON BEGAN WITH a home opener and Joq had too much on his mind at work to worry about George's blatant declaration.

Besides, he'd rationalised it away: so George was probably going to fuck Finn, so what? It's not like Joq hadn't done some serious flirting with the guys he slept with. It was nothing.

"So, you want me on the crowds too?" Alison asked.

Joq brought the monitors into focus around him. He thought of it like mapping his world: with a view of everything, he zoomed out and made a mental map of the whole, then zoomed in on one scene, then another, and another as needed.

"Yes, we'll switch this camera here from behind goals, to top tiers..." he reached past where she was sitting and showed her what he wanted. A rotating view of what was happening down there.

"Looks like our boys lost the toss, boss," Cameron said.

"Fark," Simo said and bit into a kebab. He talked around his mouthful. "That-means-ya-gonna-wan-na-watch-southern-end-in-the-fourth."

"What?" Alison asked, eyebrow raised.

Joq shook his head. "He means. Look, here," he pointed at the monitor with a view to behind goals at the southern end of the stadium. "We're gonna be kicking to this end in the fourth for goals, but you see here," he pointed at the stadium bursting with opposition supporters, "they're gonna be drunk, worked up. And well, some players can't help themselves."

"What do you mean they can't help themselves?"

"Showboating after they score, riling up the fans, that kinda thing," Cameron said. Simo nodded along, grinned.

"Fights," Simo finished.

Joq rolled his eyes. "Basically. So, you'll keep an eye on that, and you call down to security on the ground if it gets out of hand."

"Cameron keep an eye on the front, the rooms. Simo, you got everything else."

"I'll swap you for the southern end?" Simo asked Alison.

"No swapping–

"Carn—

"But you can assist and I'll work with you on everywhere else."

"Fuckin' sweet," Simo bit into his kebab and took a swig of his energy drink. Disgusting. Joq had no idea how he managed to stay skinnier than a rat in a famine.

Joq took a seat in one of the big leather chairs and leaned back in the far corner. He didn't expect much to happen, and tuned out as he listened to Simo running Alison through the various points of "potential action", a rundown of the teams, the expectation that the home team would lose, and the ongoing rivalry between the two teams.

"It's not a rivalry," Cameron said.

"It is!"

"It's not. It's a grudge match 'cos that fuckwit punched Creed out in the semis."

Joq winced at the memory, but had to agree with Cameron's take. What kind of rivalry could an original Victorian team have with a Sydney team? Victoria was the home of AFL, while Sydney was the home of gayness and the NRL. But that uppercut had been a low fucking blow and the fans still hadn't let it go. He remembered feeling like his heart stopped when George didn't get up. He'd wanted to run out of this room and onto the field. He couldn't. He'd had to settle for lurking outside the locker room after the game and asking the coach for an update since George wasn't answering his phone. Then he'd had to wait for George's sister to bring him home from the hospital later that night.

He let the memory go now as he looked at George on screen at the centre of his players, Finn near the back of the huddle. Unlike the opponent's coach, and most coaches, George wasn't yelling, he didn't even appear to be raising his voice at all, but his players were nodding, rivetted, and Joq imagined the pep talk: *focus, be in the moment. This is yours, take it.*

Joq had noticed the meditation books mixed in with the military books, and listened to George talk about his new philosophy over dinner for the last month.

The siren went and the players fanned out. The camera zoomed in on George's face as he strode for the steps that'd take him to the coach's box. He looked calm, he looked relaxed. Good.

A shame the same couldn't be said for the game. It was a shitshow from the first bounce. The only shining light was Finn. Kid got himself his first AFL goal with his first kick in his first game. Joq couldn't help his smile as Simo shouted: "Woohoo!!! We got ourselves a super-star!!!"

Finn was getting a lot of 'friendly' support from his opposition too: sharp hip and shoulders, shoves, all of it legal, off ball and out of sight of the referees. Most rookies would rise to the bait. Not Finn. Joq watched as he took each hit like it hadn't even happened.

"Well, kid's Byron, whaddya expect?" Cameron asked the room as the sole screen showing the actual game showed a close up of Finn on the field. He looked sleepy, he looked bored.

Joq soon realised that was his MO. Jogging easy as you like off the ball, eyes like a stoner, body loose, gait relaxed; then he would explode with an unpredictable moment of speed, take the mark, set up and shoot for goal or execute a perfect kick to little Lacy in the pocket.

It was tied going into half-time, which was unusual, and Joq watched as George strode out to the field and met Finn coming in. He said something and Finn grinned. It was quick, both of them turning to jog down the tunnel seconds later, but it was something.

"They seem close," Alison said.

"Nah," Simo piped up. "Coach gotta give the star some love, make him feel special. Lord knows we're fucked this season if anything happens to Flynn."

By the time they were going into the fourth, the home team was seven points down. Doable. Nothing much had happened as far as security was concerned. And nothing much, on the face of it, happened between George and Finn; although, Joq might've been the only one to notice how carefully George was controlling his expression every time the camera cut to his face after Finn made a play. It was like he was deliberately trying not to emote. Everyone caught the clenched fist pump George made when Finn got his second though, maybe not everyone realised like Joq did it was a millennium new year's level of celebration for George.

Joq tuned into Alison's monitors. Simo beat him to it.

"Yeah," he was pointing. "They probably gonna go."

He was right. And they did go—Lacy scored a beauty in the pocket and, predictably, ran at the opposition fans, thumped his chest, held his ear to listen to the boos—and it was on. The few home fans turned and laid into the rival fans hurling abuse at Lacy.

"We're going to need security, southern end…" Alison clicked on her microphone, recited the script and they watched as two security guards intervened.

She leaned back and met Joq's eyes. He nodded. Simo gave her a wild double thumbs up and she laughed.

"That's about as exciting as it gets," Cameron said.

Joq snorted.

One point in it and Finn scored another goal because of course he did. Hat trick on his first game.

Joq felt his phone buzz as he was leaving for the night.

Gonna be late. Don't wait up.

Joq unlocked his car, got in, and reminded himself of his rational-isation the whole drive home.

11

T HE BED DIPPED AS George got in and Joq groaned.

"Shh, shh," George said and kissed his nape. He smelled like whiskey and cigar smoke. "Go back to sleep."

Joq's eyes slipped shut and he went back to sleep.

When he got up early the following morning, George was dead to the world, covers kicked off, black boxers stretching over his firm ass, his broad back rising and falling with his loud breathing.

Joq went for the shower. He had an early meeting with the crew, then a late lunch on a rooftop bar with some buddies from uni. George could do... whatever George was going to do. Doing. Joq shook his head and stepped under the spray.

The lunch had been good. Really good. The twinge of disappointment Joq felt whenever he saw his old friends and one of them, inevitably, asked if he regretted turning down the offer from the Navy, the career path that would've taken him to covert ops and a pretty interesting life, barely registered anymore. He was fine with his choice, and besides, shortly after he'd moved in with George and the rest was a good history.

He pulled up to the gate full of tapas and buzzed on a few beers. The gate whirred to life and rolled aside slowly. George's car came into view, the late afternoon sun reflecting off the black paint and shining in his eyes. Joq smiled, drove in, parked behind him, got out, jogged up the steps and opened the front door.

The sound of pool water splashing made Joq grin. He kicked off his shoes, headed down the hall when he heard George's laughter—loud and quickly followed by him shouting: "I'll get you for that!" and the shriek of an answering laugh. Joq stuttered in his step.

He could see them from the kitchen through the glass windows. George was dunking Finn in a playful headlock. Finn came up and spluttered around his laughter, his eyes blinking away the water and looking up at George grinning back at him.

Joq's first thought was: this is completely inappropriate. The Head Coach cavorting alone with a rookie in his home? But as he watched Finn launch himself onto George's shoulders and use that incredible strength to push him under, the water rushing over his taut muscles and glistening in the sun, he remembered his own stupid offer. He'd gone and offered a safe fucking space. From that point of view, this was exactly what he'd invited—somewhere for Finn to come and feel welcomed, feel okay.

Joq went to the door and paused on the threshold. Finn saw him first and in that split second, Joq saw fear flash in his eyes before he leapt away from George and swam back. George spun around and looked at Joq.

"Hey," George said around a familiar smile. "Where you been?"

"Lunch," Joq replied.

"Hi, Joq," Finn said and Joq looked at him as he swam over to the edge of the pool. He was smiling now, the lazy one, like the moment before had all been in Joq's head.

"Finn," Joq nodded and forced a smile. "Good night?"

Finn laughed, his eyes on George. "It would've been, if this one didn't make me go home."

"Hey now, rook. We're one game in. Gotta save it for the finals," George swam over to him as he spoke, splashed him.

Finn was meeting him and Joq watched as another wrestling match ensued. On the face of it, it was nothing. Typical fooling around in the pool between guys. It's not like they were touching each other in a sexual way—George was planting his big palms on Finn's shoulders and pushing playfully, while Finn was clearly using his legs under the water to try and drag George under, his laughter getting caught in the water as he lost.

Joq shook his head, smiled at them and went inside to get a beer. He felt awkward. Should he join them? As he listened to their fooling around wind down to swimming and quiet chatter, he thought maybe not. He sipped his beer and thought about dinner. He'd defrosted fish for him and George. But now Finn was probably going to stay.

Fuck it, he thought as he drank his beer. If George was going to start inviting Finn over, he could bloody well cook for him.

He was going to go into the living room and watch a movie. He was definitely going to do that.

His gaze fixed on the scene in the pool: George was leaning against the edge, his arms stretched out and resting outside the water, legs kicking lazily while Finn floated on his back in front of him and watched the sky. Joq heard the murmur of their voices but couldn't make out the words. George's fond smile though, Joq could see that just fine.

He planted himself at the kitchen island, pulled out his phone, and scrolled mindlessly, his attention on the pool.

It was an hour and another beer later when they came in.

"Hey," Finn said quietly from the door.

Joq looked up. Finn was dry and dressed in shorts and a threadbare surfie hoodie, sneakers on, laces loose. If this is what he came in, then it looked like he'd rolled out of bed and headed straight over; he didn't even have a shirt on under the hoodie, his collar bones and the hollow of his throat visible.

"Heading out?" Joq asked.

George came up behind Finn, his hand brushing his side as he moved them forward.

"Gonna give Finn a lift," George said.

"Oh, you didn't want to stay for dinner?" Joq heard himself asking.

"Nah," Finn smiled. It wasn't a real smile and in that moment Joq knew Finn knew the dinner invitation was more like an invitation not to stay for dinner. "Me and the other rookies gonna game and order in."

"No junk," George said, smiling at Finn. "See you when I get back," he shot over his shoulder.

"See ya," Finn said with a little wave.

And then they were gone.

Dinner was on the table by the time George came back.

"Hey," he said as he came in and went for the fridge.

"Hey," Joq replied. "All good?"

George shut the fridge and came over to the table with his water. "Yeah, you know, rookies," he grinned and kissed Joq's temple as he went past him for his seat.

"Yeah," Joq breathed out, embarrassingly grateful for the contact.

George gave him a pointed look as he sat.

"What?" Joq asked.

"I didn't," George started. Then looked at his dinner. "This looks good."

"You didn't what?"

George picked up his utensils, cut into the fish, heaped salad on top of it. His eyes were on the fork suspended in the air when he answered. "With him. I didn't. It's a bad idea," he said and took a mouthful.

Joq was nodding, because it was, but he felt oddly disappointed as well. Did he want to get this self-righteous thing over George? No, that was ridiculous. Why would he want that?

"It is," he replied as firmly as he could and focused on his food.

George grunted, asked about lunch and they moved on.

12

FINN HAD A SLUMP after that. Three games and he couldn't buy a point. He had an absolute clanger in one of them—right in front of goal, perfect angle, no wind; he booted it out of bounds on the full. Joq felt bad for him. The kid's raging crush on his boyfriend aside, Finn seemed like a genuinely nice guy.

The media were brutal. Social media was worse. But looking at Finn, you'd never know it—sure, he looked tighter around the eyes when the cameras zoomed in on his face after another miss, but other than that, he was the same calm player, loose, smile coming easy at his team mates when they jogged up to him, tapped him on the ass and gave him platitudes.

Joq only knew it was getting to him because he was on the phone with George all the time. At least, Joq assumed George was talking to Finn when he got up to take a call in another room while he and Joq watched TV or ate dinner.

Or he was in their living room, Joq thought dryly as he came home from work after the third game to the sound of George's soft voice: "You gotta get out of your head, it's all up here." George tapped Finn's temple gently while Finn nodded, his eyes fixed on the carpet.

"Hey," Joq said from the hallway.

George and Finn jumped, heads turning as one. George was sitting on the coffee table, Finn on the couch in front of him.

"Sorry," Joq said.

"All good," George straightened out of his huddle. "Didn't hear you come in."

"Hey, Joq," Finn reclined back in the cushions, his smile tired.

"Wouldn't worry about the game. This one had some clangers in his time," Joq nodded his head at George and smiled.

Finn smiled back and George snorted, but their combined reactions felt forced—Joq got the distinct feeling they wanted him to go away, that his opinion as someone who'd never played was not to be taken seriously.

"Well, I'm gonna," he waved his hand at the kitchen. "You guys want anything?"

"I'm good," George smiled.

"Nah. Thanks, Joq."

"Okay."

Joq left them to it. He got himself a cider, went over to the sliding door, opened it, looked out, then closed it firmly without going outside. His feet were quiet on the tiles as he crept back into the kitchen, stood on the other side of the wall from the living room. He listened.

"I should go," Finn said.

"You don't have to," George replied.

Finn sighed. The couch creaked and Joq imagined him sitting up again.

"No, I should... leave you to it."

"What I want to be left to is getting my best player out of his head," George said. Joq could practically see his gruff smile around the words.

"Yeah," Finn's reply was quiet. And miserable. "Can't let everyone down."

"Hey now," George's tone shifted to serious. "Fuck everyone."

Joq's eyes widened. That was more vehement than it needed to be.

"This is about you," George went on in the same tone. "You gotta realise one bad game, hell, fifty bad games doesn't change who you are."

"Think fifty bad games is gonna change who I am," Finn replied.

"No, it doesn't. Fifty great games, fifty bad ones. You're still—"

"Still a pretty boy wanker who should spend less time cruising for pussy and cock with his thirst traps and more time playing actual football?"

George sucked in a breath. "I told you not to read about yourself online," he said after a minute, curt.

"Yeah, well, it's probably true," Finn sounded defeated.

"That's why you post that shit?" Now George sounded angry.

"Of course not."

"Then why'd you say it's true?"

"I dunno, lots of people message me about it."

"Is that what you want? To meet a guy that way?"

"What? No! Of course not."

"'Cos you're not gonna meet someone worthy of you if he's reaching out just 'cos of some picture."

Finn snorted. "Pretty sure I'm not gonna meet a guy anytime soon. And I dunno about worthy of me," Joq could practically see the air quotes, could hear the sarcasm dripping in Finn's tone. "They're right. I'm just a dumb fuck-up with a nice face and good abs who could've been good at football if he spent more time on it and less on his fucking image."

Joq waited for George to counter with a big speech about self-esteem and not going online. He sipped his cider.

"You gotta know any guy who gets you is gonna be the luckiest son of a bitch in the world," George said.

Joq almost choked.

"Stop trying to make me feel better."

"I'm not."

Joq could hear them breathing as silence descended.

"You're a great player," George went on after several beats. "And yeah, you're easy on the eyes. But that's not all you are. That's not what makes you... special."

"What makes me special?" Finn's voice was so low, Joq barely caught it.

"This," George replied softly, his body shifting like he was moving. "And this."

Joq wanted to peek so badly, but he couldn't. Not from this angle with the lights on in there.

"No one can touch this," George finished quietly. "Not unless you let them."

Joq could hear them breathing, could hear the sound of Finn moving on the couch, but he didn't say anything.

"And no fuckwit on some social media site is fucking worthy of it, you hear me?"

Finn laughed and Joq felt the tension break. George's tone shifted back to the Coach vibe as he started talking about Finn's actual game, and Joq backed up, crept outside.

It was Monday morning after that, after the latest disaster of a game, though the team won anyway, be pretty embarrassing if they didn't against a bottom side team from the West, and Joq was screwing the lid on his takeaway mug before he headed to work when the intercom at the gate went. George had the day off, which meant he was down below in the gym.

Joq figured it was a delivery and went to answer the intercom but George beat him to it.

"*Yeah?*"

"*It's me,*" Finn's voice crackled over the speaker.

Joq heard the click of the gate opening.

"*In the gym,*" George said.

Joq slung his backpack over his shoulder, grabbed his coffee and went into the living room. He peered through the curtain and watched as Finn came up the long driveway. He had his hands jammed in his pockets, shoulders hunched, his gaze fixed on a point ahead as his mouth started to curve into a reluctant smile.

George appeared, his arms coming up as Finn got closer. He wrapped him in a tight hug. Finn's hands stayed in his pockets, but he brought his head down and rested it on George's shoulder, sagging into the embrace. George was clearly saying something, Finn moving his head from side to side, rubbing his face on the fabric of George's singlet before dragging his face up the bare skin of his throat. His lips moved against George's ear and Joq felt something twist in his gut when George gripped Finn tighter.

He stepped back and let the curtain flutter closed. George had said he wasn't going to do anything and Joq believed him. Finn was, understandably, upset. He was also young, away from home. George was comforting him. There was no way anything else was going on because Joq got that George got that it was a fucking terrible idea.

Joq stayed rooted to the spot anyway. He didn't want to interrupt. He was going to be late. He was starting to get pretty fucking mad when he heard the sound of their footsteps heading up the driveway, heading for the open garage that led into the gym.

By the time he went out, every movement felt like a pretence of normal since he knew they hadn't closed the door and would see him as he got into his car. He wasn't sure why he was the one feeling so self-conscious; but ever since Finnegan Flynn stepped down that tunnel, Joq felt himself turning into an uncertain version of himself.

He clicked the immobiliser and couldn't stop himself from glancing up at the garage. Finn and George were turning to him and all three of them froze as if caught. Nobody was doing anything unusual—Joq had his hand on the car door; George had his hand on Finn's elbow; and Finn was staring wide-eyed with his arm in George's grip.

"Heading out?" George asked.

"Work," Joq croaked.

"Have fun," Finn said, his smile too wide. He was stepping back as he said it and George was letting him go.

"Yep," Joq said and got into the car.

He felt shaky as he got the car started, clicked the gate open, and looked over his shoulder. He was almost too scared to look back. To see George's face plastered in a fake smile, Finn looking twitchy beside him, both of them moving to wave goodbye. He was beginning to think he'd played this all wrong—he should've told George to go on and fuck the kid, get it out of his system until they realised there was nothing more there than physical attraction.

Joq looked back up the driveway as he spun the wheel to reverse out onto the road. No one was looking his way. George had his back to the driveway, his big body shielding Finn from view.

13

G EORGE WAS PARTICULARLY ACCOMMODATING when Joq got home that night. Joq wanted to think it was because George was going away later in the week—away game in the West to play Fremantle, who, unlike the other team out there, could be contenders this year—and George always got handsy before he went on the road. Joq used to think it was because he picked up whenever George went away and George liked hearing about it, in explicit detail, as soon as he got back. It got him all worked up and they'd fuck about it. It was fun.

But because of what'd happened that morning with Finn, and what had been running through Joq's head all day at work about what might be happening at home, he couldn't get into it.

"What's with you?" George asked the third time Joq moved away after George came up behind him and caged him in against the bench.

"Nothin'," Joq spun around, a few inches between them. "Just, not feeling it, I guess."

George raised both eyebrows. "You?"

Joq cracked a smile and looked at his feet.

"You already get some today or something?"

It was a joke, but there was an accusation in there too. It made Joq look up and defend himself.

"Of course not. What? You think I'm double teaming Cameron and Simo at work?"

George screwed his face up, and Joq couldn't help himself—he laughed and George chuckled with him.

"Sorry," Joq said as he settled down. "I'm just," he waved his hand around. What was he just? All mixed up in his fucking head about this shit.

George nodded like he got it. "All good, just, road trip," he shrugged and moved away.

"Later?" Joq straightened.

"Sure, babe," George said over his shoulder as he grabbed his phone and went into the living room.

Joq went out to the pool and told himself to get his shit together.

Practice was brutal that week, as Joq saw firsthand and heard about in great detail from George at home.

"Fit. They need to outrun those guys. That team," he shook his head as he paced while Joq sat on the couch and listened while also trying to see his show on the TV. "They're in the sweet spot, you know? Perfect fitness, all averaging around twenty-four..."

The next day, Joq watched the team on the monitors coming back down the tunnel, looking destroyed, and he knew it was because George was making them run "laps, laps, laps."

Finn was near the back. He looked exhausted, but he was smiling, taking the hip and shoulder from one of the veterans with a laugh. George came down the tunnel behind them, glancing from his clipboard to his team. Joq rubbed his jaw as he watched them. They'd fly out after everyone had showered and changed into their suits.

"Not much doin', boss," Simo said.

"Nope, head out if you want," Joq said.

"You sure?"

"Yeah, I'll finish it off."

"Awesome, thanks," Simo was getting up and packing all his shit into his backpack, clattering around.

"Later, boss," he said as he went out the door.

"Later," Joq said to the sound of the door clicking shut. The room descended into the kind of silence only possible after someone like Simo left it.

He watched the monitors. The players were heading into the showers. The support crew were packing their gear. The media room was filling with reporters for the pre-flight press conference. Joq glanced around at the other monitors—the stadium was empty like a ghost house, a cavernous space of empty seats, the field filling with seagulls under the lights.

Joq picked up his pen and flicked it in a rhythm on his notepad. He needed to make a note about the upcoming roster; he needed to train a backup for two weeks' time when Cameron went on leave because his missus was having a baby; he needed to call maintenance about a camera outside the trainer's room that was broken. His eyes kept drifting back to the monitors in the locker room.

The players were back in the room, in various states of getting dressed, and Joq sought out Finn. He was near the back, pants on, feet bare, turning to grab his shirt. Joq had seen enough athletes to not get worked up about their physical perfection, but he could appreciate Finn was in great shape. It was accentuated by his genetic gifts—incredible broad shoulders, thick biceps, an impressive chest. He was going to grow into a monster of a man. He was laughing at something one of the other guys was saying to him, at ease, even though it must've been weighing on him: to start out so well and then do nothing. Still, like George said, in the scheme of a career, a few games was nothing. Joq guessed, looking at Finn buttoning up his shirt, his smile not dimming as he looked down, he was actually listening to that.

George appeared in the room, suit on, and said something. Joq watched as Finn gave him a grateful look. The captain and Lacy followed George out to face the media.

Joq continued to tap his pen. He should pack up and head out. He needed to set the alarms. He had no reason to stay.

He watched as the players left in pairs, in groups, headed down the tunnel for the bus to the airport. Finn was still sitting, fiddling with his tie, then rummaging through his bag. He zipped it up, looked around the empty room, and went back to his tie, pulling the smaller part out and then tucking it back in.

Joq was still tapping his pen when George returned.

Finn stood.

Joq's hand stilled as he watched George walk over to him. He'd give his left nut to hear what they were saying, but as he leaned closer, he noticed they weren't speaking at all, they were just standing a few inches apart and looking at each other.

Oddly, it was George who broke first; shaking his head in a self-deprecating way and dropping his gaze. Finn's lips parted like he was about to say something. George looked up at him, leaned forward. Finn went still, but George went for Finn's bag. Their chests brushed and they startled away from each other.

Joq could make out the apology Finn was giving in the way his lips moved, the nervous way his hand ran through his hair. He watched as George shouldered his bag, said something and headed for the door, Finn close behind him a beat later.

And what the fuck was that? Joq wondered as he watched them fall into step with each other, George giving Finn a gentle shoulder nudge as they headed up the tunnel for the bus.

A WAY GAMES DIDN'T ALWAYS give Joq the chance to watch at home, the stadium often booked for other sports and events, but this Saturday was free and he took the opportunity to watch from the comfort of his living room.

It was wet. The rain coming down sideways, the wind blowing so hard the players' hair whipped around their faces.

Joq settled in with a beer and smiled when they showed George at the centre of the huddle, his hand moving as he spoke to the players, looked at each guy in turn.

"Here's hoping he's telling Flynn the aim of the game is to score…"

Joq leaned forward and clicked mute. He always gave the commentators the benefit of the doubt, and they always managed to piss him off within the first minute. Finn might not be his favourite person, but this was still his team, George was still his man, and in a weird way hearing the insult made him like Finn more. Not that he didn't like Finn; he didn't know him well enough to outright dislike him, and while he certainly felt uneasy with whatever was brewing between him and George, he honestly assumed it would end up just being a fuck. He'd been with George for so long, the thought of them breaking up was unimaginable.

But that weird moment in the locker room had tipped his unease into something he couldn't decipher, even to himself.

Lying in bed the night before, he'd scrolled through his possible hook-ups, read messages and invites to meet up from new guys, and then tossed his phone aside, turned the lamp off, and stayed awake thinking about it for a long time.

Seeing the camera focus on Finn now brought all those unsettled thoughts back. He watched as the players fanned out across the ground, the camera on Finn, his hair wet and plastered to the side of his head, his expression neutral as he jogged to his spot beyond the centre bounce. The veteran defender they had on him was already shoving him, and Finn was doing his usual Teflon routine like it wasn't even happening. He was good at that, Joq thought, acting like nothing was going on when clearly something was going on.

The ball was bounced at the centre and the game was on. Joq tried to shake off his thoughts and simply watch the game. George would want to talk about it when he got back, and Joq rarely got a chance to give it his full attention.

But what had Finn been waiting for? Did he understand what an open relationship was? The operative word being 'relationship.' Even if George did do something with him, it'd just be fucking. But Finn had been looking at George like he expected something.

And he was back on camera now as he scooped up the water logged ball one-handed, evaded his defender with that characteristic explosion of speed, brought his saturated boot up and kicked a belter from the top of the fifty metre mark. It sailed through the centre of the goal. His team mates were jumping on him in a mob, the shot a close-up of his face as he laughed.

They cut to George in the box. He had his mouth covered as he spoke to the assistant coach, but Joq could see his eyes were crinkled and he wondered if he was covering what he was saying, knowing the cameras were on him, or covering his smile.

Joq finished his beer and got another one. By half time, Joq was three beers in and clicking it off. They'd win—no way Fremantle could beat them in these conditions, they sucked in the wet—and Finn had already scored another goal. Joq wanted to be happy for him, but he felt the camera cuts between Finn's beaming face and George's carefully hidden one were taunting him.

He picked up his phone and resolved to get laid after all. There was a cute young guy less than ten kilometres away, and Joq had initially resisted his advances given his age. Now he was thinking twenty-four hardly seemed that young compared to Joq's thirty-three, given his boyfriend was currently getting cruised by a twenty-year-old.

Hey, busy?

He hit send and told himself he was not going to think about Finn or anything related to it until he had to see their smiling faces when they got back.

Always got time 4 U baby.

Joq snorted and got his shit together.

15

"**D**ID YOU SEE IT?" were the first words out of George's mouth when he got into Joq's car at the airport the following evening.

"Some of it," Joq said and turned to check oncoming traffic in the airport pick-up lane. "Nice win."

"Win? We destroyed them."

"It was wet," Joq said as he pulled out.

"Wet doesn't account for a score like that, come on."

Joq glanced at him. George was looking out the windscreen, clasping the hand rest, a contented glow radiating off him. Joq didn't know why it pissed him off so much.

"Yeah, well, do it when it's not wet and I'll be impressed."

George scoffed. "You switch teams while I was away?"

"No," Joq sped up and changed lanes as they got onto the highway. "I'm just sayin'."

"What's with you? Didn't you just get laid? You hung up after two minutes last night," George squeezed his thigh and it was normal; the teasing tone, the invitation to discuss it, to get the foreplay started while they were still in the car.

It pissed Joq off even more. "No, I did," he glanced at George, who was smiling warmly back at him. Joq couldn't have explained why he said what he did next. "Did you?"

"What?"

"Did you get laid?"

"Of course not. Jesus, Joq," George said.

Joq peered at him. George was enraged and offended in equal measure.

"Sorry, I don't know why I—

"I said I wasn't..."

Joq could feel those eyes on him, feel the anger, but George didn't go on.

"I know," Joq said after nothing but George's bursts of breathing filled the space between them.

Joq glanced at him. George turned in his seat so he was looking out the window.

"He's too young," George said, clipped. "He's on the team."

"I know," Joq said again. He really wanted to add that Finn had a crush so big it was obvious from space, but he bit his tongue. He didn't want to admit, even in his own head, it was clear George had the same meteor-sized crush.

"Nothing happened. Nothing's happening," George went on.

Joq felt uneasy again. *The man doth protest too much*...

"Babe," he said gently, "I know."

George nodded, a sharp jerk of his head.

"So, what about you then? Another suit?" George was forcing calm and interest into his voice. Joq recognised it for the peace offering it was.

He didn't know why he lied. "Yeah," he replied and carefully did not think about the young guy he'd fucked until the early hours of this morning.

"Any good?"

Joq smiled over at him. "Meh, he was alright…"

George laughed and Joq felt them settle back onto familiar, safe ground as he wound back into their suburb and wound George up with a made-up story of a hook-up with a guy his own age.

By the time they were falling into bed to fuck, hands and mouths moving into practised position, it felt the same as it always had. Mostly. But as George rolled Joq onto his hands and knees, lined up and pushed in, Joq couldn't shake the feeling of someone else in the room with them. And not in the sexy fantasy way.

As he slid to his elbows and peered back at George behind him, he saw his eyes were shut tightly, his breathing laboured, his thrusts desperate and erratic. Joq couldn't shake the feeling it was both him George was fucking, and yet not him at the same time.

16

JOQ NEEDED TO HUSTLE if he was going to make it to George's birthday party before it went beyond fashionably late. Not that it mattered all that much—he was just a buddy at these things, and not even the publicly-deemed closest one. He'd made his peace with that.

"Hey, got a minute?" Alison asked as he was packing his laptop into his bag.

"Sure," he smiled over at her as he zipped up.

"It's just, I need. Well, the thing is," she was literally wringing her hands. Her normally composed, plain features twisting up.

"If you hate it here and need to quit, it's okay," Joq smiled at her reassuringly. It happened. The work was dull. He'd need to find someone else though, and soon with Cameron going on leave.

"No, no," she shook her head. "I just, my mother got herself kicked out of her current place. Again. And I need this weekend—

"You need the weekend off?" Joq hoisted his bag. "No problem."

She stopped speaking and clicked her mouth shut.

"Really?"

"Course, I'll cover it," he said and went by her. "I gotta run now. You still good to do on call with security tonight?"

"Of course," she smiled. "Thanks, Joq. Really, thanks. My mum..." she shook her head, gave him a wry smile. He got it.

He started to push out the door. "It's really fine, and it's really none of my business. You need time off, you can take time off."

He heard her say thanks again as the door slipped closed. He really needed to hustle.

The party was at its peak when he got there. They'd booked a private room on the top floor of a swanky bar overlooking the Yarra River, the water like black ink catching the reflection of a hundred dotted lights outside the windows. The room was chic on the surface, but it had pool tables and dart boards, a wider beer selection than necessary, and party food to George's taste—mini sausage rolls, party pies, quiche and prawn cocktails—which all combined to take the sheen off the classiness. Joq always gave George shit for his taste—was he not aware the world had moved on to sliders and canapés? George shrugged and muttered about how he liked what he liked and it was his party, he wasn't "no fashionista." This made Joq snort; he couldn't believe George knew that word.

He sought out the man of the hour now as the security guard let him in through the roped off area. His eyes landed on Finn instead. Finn was laughing, eyes bright, his mouth moving in response to something Lacy was saying to him at the bar, their other teammates around them. Finn settled into a warm smile as Lacy replied, but his gaze moved to somewhere else in the room. Joq followed it.

George. Standing with his sister. She was saying something, but he was looking away from her, his head lifting to look back at Finn as if he felt the gaze land on him. He smiled back, then returned his attention to his sister.

Joq went for the bar on the opposite side of Finn and his crew. The latest craft pale ale in hand, he made his way through the crowds over to George. But George was gone. Cara was still there.

"Joaquin," she said around a familiar smile. "It's so good to see you."

He leaned down to kiss her cheek. "Cara, how are you?"

"Eh, you know, happy to get a night off," she winked.

"I bet," he indulged her. "What're they now? Six, seven?"

She bumped him. "Four."

Her twin boys were the adorable terrors George had hoped would placate his parents' disappointment their first born was gay and thus, in their minds, unlikely to have kids of his own, to have the white wedding they seemed to envision as the crowning glory on top of his incredible success. Oh, they were nice about it. But Joq didn't miss the shared looks, the flashes of grief whenever they visited; as if Joq's presence in George's home confirmed, again and again, some immeasurable loss.

"He's looking good," Cara said and smiled over at the bar.

Joq looked at George. He was with one of his assistants and Scotty. A fellow player, now retired, Scotty and George came into the league together, played their whole careers together, and retired together. George was holding his beer loosely, grinning as he listened to Scotty talk and gesticulate wildly. He was probably telling an embellished fishing story that occurred near his property in Far North Queensland.

"He is," Joq confirmed.

He glanced over at Finn again. He didn't know why. Finn wasn't doing anything special—playing a game of pool with Lacy. Or, well, trying to. Lacy was wasted, which was pretty standard. George always said the only reason Lacy managed to avoid getting pulled up for it was it never affected his game, his training, or his attitude—on the face of it, he was a model player, so, what could you do?

Joq watched now as Lacy said something that made Finn's eyes widen. Finn shook his head, and Lacy skulked off to the bathroom.

"George said you've been good for Finn too?"

Joq turned to look down at her. "Really?"

"Something about a dinner," she shrugged and flagged down a waiter with a tray of prawn cocktails. Joq shook his head vehemently. Disgusting.

"Yeah, thought he could use a proper welcome," Joq managed to get out. He focused on Finn again because it seemed like Cara was waiting for him to do so.

Finn was lining up a pool cue, rocking it back and forth between his fingers on the table, his eyes focused, his body a long line of muscle bent over the table.

"George was worried about him, having to deal with that injury and then leaving his mum and sister."

Finn struck the balls and leaned back as one almost went down a pocket before ricocheting out. Lacy reappeared behind him, sniffing so obviously Joq wondered why he didn't just do the coke on the bar. He watched as Lacy took the pool cue from Finn and bumped him aside.

"Yeah, George loves to worry," he smiled at her.

She tilted her head. "I never thought he'd be that kinda coach though."

"Hmmm," Joq was looking back at the game. Lacy was refusing to let Finn take his shot after he'd shanked it so badly, he was lucky he hadn't ripped the table. He saw George come over and grab the pool cue out of his hand from behind.

He didn't hand it to Finn. Lacy complained half-heartedly, but stepped aside when George stepped up and smirked at Finn.

"You know, these are his men. These are men," she went on, laughing.

Joq wanted to look at her, but he was rivetted by George lining up a shot; he looked completely focused on the play, and yet, something about the way his body angled towards Finn—this play was for him.

"And I'm not saying Finn's not a man. He is. Have you seen his social media? I'm a married woman, but damn," Cara reached for a glass of champagne from another waiter walking by.

"I've seen it," Joq nodded, eyes on the pool table.

"But the way George carried on about him since he got drafted," she took a long sip.

George struck the white ball and sunk two in opposite corner pockets, the cracking sound loud from the other side of the room.

"You'd think Finn had been drafted to go to war," she huffed a short laugh.

George stretched to his full height and strolled past Finn, smiling indulgently before he lined up for his next shot. Finn's lips were twisted to the side in a playful smile, his lips moving as he muttered something. George snorted with laughter. He pushed his hair back off his face as he rounded the end of the table.

"It was nice though, seeing how much he cared."

George lined up the next shot. Glanced up at Finn. He winked and took the shot without dropping eye contact.

"I didn't think he'd be like that…"

The balls ricocheted around the table, the clunk of more falling loud in the room.

Finn said something and Joq knew it was to ask if he was ever going to get another shot.

George was grinning at him, then coming over to stand close by Finn's side. His hands were on top of the pool cue as he surveyed his options for the eight ball. He reached out with the cue and pointed at the bottom corner pocket.

"He's been good for him."

Finn was shaking his head, a disbelieving smile on his face.

"Who, Finn?" Joq asked.

"Yeah."

George was leaning over to take the shot. Joq looked at Finn watching him.

"Given him a lot of confidence," she said.

Joq snorted. "Don't think George needs help in that department."

He could feel her quizzical look beside him, but he was stuck on Finn's expression—impressed, yes, but fond too.

Her silence stretched and he was forced to look at her or risk committing a social faux pas.

"George is about the most confident guy I know," he said.

He heard the balls crack and glanced back.

George had sunk the eight ball and as he tossed the cue on the table and moved at the same time, he smiled at Finn. Finn shook his head. George ruffled his hair as he went by and Finn asked for a rematch.

Fortunately, Scotty came over and scooped up the cue and told George he was about to get his ass kicked. "No more taunting the rookies!"

George laughed and his face shifted to the way he usually looked at the guys. That was not how he looked at Finn.

Finn was taking a seat at the bar. Lacy was next to him, mouth moving. Finn giggled, his big body shaking, and George looked up from racking the balls and smiled softly at him.

"Even George needs someone to tell him that sometimes," Cara said. It was bordering on critical.

Joq looked at her, chastised.

"Believe me, I tell him. I think maybe your parents could've stepped up a bit more in that department," he replied and couldn't believe himself. It was fucking Finn. Watching Finn moon all over George; it made him mad, and now he was taking it out on Cara.

She looked surprised.

"I know they haven't been the best," she started.

"I'm sorry, I shouldn't have said that. It's not—

"No, it's. It hasn't been fair on him. On either of you."

"We really don't have to discuss it."

"Okay," she said after a moment, her gaze travelling over to George kicking Scotty's ass at pool. "I'm just glad to see him happy now."

And what the fuck did that mean?

"Yeah," he breathed out. "He's good. I'm gonna... beer. You good?"

"Yes, thank you," she smiled, still warm, still familiar, but Joq had an uneasy feeling he'd played that all wrong.

Joq was beginning to feel like it was the party that wouldn't end. He was stuck talking to management, his beer going warm in his hand. He shot another look over to where George was still playing rounds of pool with Scotty and some of the older guys. Lacy was long gone, and Finn was nowhere in sight. He wanted to leave with George, but he'd had enough.

He excused himself and went to put his beer on the bar near the service entrance. Finn bumped into him as he came out of the toilet.

"Sorry, sorry," Finn said and looked up. The apology was still coming when he saw it was Joq and his face contorted before smoothing into an embarrassed smile. "Joq, hey. Didn't know you were still here."

"I didn't know you knew I was here at all," Joq replied, smiling a tad insolently, but also to soften the remark.

"Well, it's George's birthday, so," Finn smiled back weakly.

"It is," Joq replied. "Heading out?"

"Uh, yeah?" Finn looked at him like he couldn't comprehend why he was asking.

No, Joq thought as he sized him up, like he interpreted that as an accusation.

"George and Scotty will make this an all-nighter," Joq said.

Finn shrugged like he didn't give a shit either way. The little liar. Well, he was hardly little, but he was young enough to deserve the tag.

Joq placed his beer on the bar.

"What about you?" Finn asked.

Joq met his eyes from where he was leaning past him to get to the bar.

"What about me what?"

Finn jerked his chin. "Heading out?"

Joq got the weirdest feeling this conversation was all happening in subtext. He felt like there was a wrong answer and a right answer.

And fuck that.

"Yeah," he said slowly and straightened. "George knows where his bed is," he glanced over at him. George was watching Scotty take a shot and giving him pointers like he couldn't help himself. Scotty guffawed and shook his head at him.

Joq glanced back at Finn.

Finn's lips were twisted and the alcohol must've loosened him up because he wasn't doing the usual, 'I'm super chill with everything' routine. No, he was mad.

Joq leaned forward, leaned in for the kill. "He gets a bit worked up after nights like this."

He felt Finn jerk away from him. Joq huffed a laugh.

He expected Finn's anger to be dialled right up.

He didn't expect the hurt look.

"You know how it is," he added lamely and wished he'd walked away after the previous comment.

"You shouldn't be telling me this," Finn said. There was an attempt at authority in his voice, but he couldn't quite cover the wounded lilt.

"You do know what boyfriends do, right?" Joq didn't know why he was pushing it, but he wasn't about to stop.

Another hurt look flashed in Finn's eyes. "That's George's business."

Joq raised both eyebrows at him. And alright, kid's got some claws after all.

"I think I know what George's business is better than you do," he replied.

Finn exhaled noisily. He looked young. His face was blotchy and red, his anger simmering like he wanted to explode. It was quite disorientating.

"Hey," drawled from behind him.

George. Drunk and happy. That shifted fast when he looked over Joq's shoulder. "Finn?" he asked, eyes sharpening. "You okay?"

Joq watched Finn nod quickly and school his expression to neutral, smile close-mouthed. "All good, heading out."

"You sure?"

"We should probably go too," Joq turned to George as he spoke. But George was shaking his head.

"Me and Scotty going to the casino. Was gonna see if you guys wanted?"

"No, I'm beat—" Joq said just as Finn said, "Yeah, sure."

And fuck it all.

"Awesome," George said to Finn over Joq's shoulder, smiling the radiant smile of the inebriated. "You sure?" George leaned back to ask Joq.

Joq didn't want to go. He didn't want to leave George with Finn either.

"Do you really think that's a good idea?" he asked.

"Yes, Mum," George laughed.

Joq ground his teeth. "No," he said slowly. He hated talking to drunk people, and George was particularly irritating when he was pissed. "I mean all those people? Camera phones? You," he looked around, just Scotty left, "three in a public place?"

George frowned, his drunk mind working through it.

"I'm sure it'll be fine," Finn said.

"What'll be fine?" Scotty asked as he came over and threw an arm over George and Joq. "Joqqy!" he yelled in Joq's face.

"The casino—

"Hell to the yeah!" Scotty cut him off.

"You wanna get your picture taken throwing up in a gutter?" Joq asked.

Scotty frowned.

Finn scoffed.

Joq shot him a look.

"We can go to George's! You still got the dart board?"

"Yeah!" George grinned at Scotty, then looked at Finn. "Finn?"

Joq wanted to say no one was playing fucking darts.

17

♥

EVERYONE WAS PLAYING FUCKING darts, and it really was the night that wouldn't end. Maybe he should've asked Lacy for a line of his coke. As he watched Finn doubling over with laughter at something George said, George smiling all pleased at the reaction, he thought maybe he should've asked Lacy for some of his harder stuff—everyone knew he took ecstasy and rolled on the regular. It was a mystery how he stayed so good, evaded the testers. Joq rubbed his eyes and right then didn't really give a shit; he'd take the good stuff and be not here.

He sipped his soda water and watched them play. Scotty kept rubbing Finn on the head every time Finn got the right point on the board, which made Finn giggle and bat at his hands playfully. George nudged Scotty away every time he did it. Scotty laughed at George like the whole thing was hilarious. Finn blushed and hid his face in his hair, carefully not looking at Joq on the couch on the other side of the room.

After a while, Scotty dropped down on the couch next to him, stretching one arm behind him, spilling the bourbon and coke in his other hand.

"Joqqy!" he said.

"Scotty," Joq replied.

"Your boy looks good, eh?"

Joq snorted. Scotty always did like to press the gay joke angle on their friendship. If only he knew.

"Ya know, I always reckoned he had a bit of a thing for you," Scotty took a loud slurp of his drink. "Not anymore!" he laughed and Joq followed his gaze to George and Finn playing darts.

There was so much to unpack there, Joq wasn't sure where to start.

"A thing for me? C'mon, man," Joq shook his head. "Enough with the gay jokes, eh? You know I am."

Scotty squinted at him. "Yeah, course I know that," he jerked his chin at George. "So's George, but like, you know that." His eyes widened. "You know that, right?"

"How do you know that?"

Scotty looked at him like he was fucking stupid. "You reckon I don't know my best mate?"

"No, that's not..." Joq shook his head. "He told you?" George never told him that.

They turned as one when there was a crashing sound followed by glass smashing, Finn's laughter and George's "Shit, rook."

George's framed jersey from his rookie year was a shattered mess on the floor. George was giggling and looking from Finn to the mess.

Joq didn't want to know. And he was pretending he didn't live here, so, he wasn't cleaning that up.

"He told you?" he asked Scotty again.

"What?" Scotty tilted his head, his out of control black hair all over the place. "Oh, nah. I figured it out." He shrugged, gulped down his drink.

"How?"

"Well," Scotty gave him a sly smile. "He was always checking you out when we were rookies."

Joq felt himself blush, which was stupid. Of course George checked him out—they were fucking whenever George could get past his irrational fear of being discovered in Joq's shitty share-house in Brunswick.

"And then there was that rumour plus all the gay porn in his apartment," Scotty laughed. "Always thought you guys would hook up."

Joq shrugged. What else could he do? He and George had lived together for ten fucking years, but George still made sure they kept it on the down-low by only allowing "couple shit" upstairs and in their bedroom. Joq knew the deal going in, he still knew the deal. He didn't love it, but he did love George.

"Guess not," Scotty drained his drink as he nodded at George and Finn. They were crouched down over the mess, picking up the glass and snickering like idiots.

Scotty was getting up to get himself another drink, the couch dipping awkwardly as his bulk left it—he'd packed it on since he retired, not fat, but certainly one big, beast of a man now, the ruckman height and build lending itself to the 'farmer's build' as he liked to call it. Joq wasn't even sure what he was farming up there. Marijuana probably. But not a salient point right now.

George's crush on Finn, and Finn's hard on for George was so obvious, even Scotty assumed they were together?

Joq stood up. No one seemed to notice. He went up the steps into the main house. He didn't know what to do with himself. He could still hear them—their voices loud over the Top 40 shit Finn put on when he arrived, George and Scotty ribbing him mercilessly with matching grins.

Joq shook his head. He went and sat on the couch, clicked on the TV.

The glow from the TV was still on, the volume low, when he woke to the sound of someone opening the door outside the games room, coming through the door. He heard voices. Joq was barely awake, but he woke up fast with tension ricocheting through his body—surely they wouldn't, not here, not in their home!

"Just a few more steps," Scotty said.

Joq sighed inwardly, the relief so profound he felt like he actually deflated.

"Where's Finn?" George slurred as he and Scotty rounded the bottom of the stairs, their big bodies black masses against the blue of the night in the house.

Scotty chuckled. "You got it bad, bro."

"It's not like that," George said.

"Sure it's not," Scotty laughed and helped George up the stairs.

"Is he alright?"

"Put him in an Uber myself."

"No funny business, ya hear me?"

Joq heard a scuffle.

"Fuck's sake George, I ain't trying to get on that dick. Jesus."

Joq listened to them breathing. He wondered if George would remember he had a fucking boyfriend he might assume was up there in that bed.

"Fuck, I'm drunk," George said after a minute.

"Yep, bed, c'mon."

"Don't fucking..." George trailed off, he sounded tired. He sounded serious.

Scotty sighed. "I'm not. I got my own... mess."

"Good."

Scotty laughed. "Thanks, buddy."

They reached the upstairs landing and Joq clicked the TV off. Scotty would take the spare room so Joq would sleep down here. He felt a surge of anger, but then a hysterical laugh bubbled up—pretending he was the buddy crashing downstairs on the couch was the least of his problems right now.

18

"GEORGE," JOQ SHOOK HIS shoulder.

George groaned, buried his face in the pillow. Joq felt a fresh surge of anger.

"George, you need to get Scotty out of here," he hissed and shook him again.

"Joq?' George rolled over. He was squinting against the mid-morning sunshine streaming through the open windows.

Who else would it be?

"My parents are coming over for lunch," Joq couldn't hide his irritation at George not remembering, at him being hungover as fuck when he knew this lunch was today.

"Cool, yeah," George rubbed his eyes. "He'll be gone by then."

"I need to start cooking now," Joq hoped George picked up on how stupid Joq currently thought he was.

"Okay," George groaned, rolled over and buried his face back in the pillow.

"Okay, well, I'm gonna start that and you can explain to Scotty why I'm in your kitchen cooking lunch for my parents," Joq got up and felt an illicit thrill at the thought of it. It wasn't the worst idea.

George huffed. The blankets were thrown off dramatically, and he stumbled out of the door ahead of Joq, slamming it shut behind him.

Joq took a deep breath and sat on the bed. The room reeked of alcohol and he hated the thought of George in this state around his parents. It wasn't worth having an argument about, so he resolved to stew on it silently while he waited. He could hear them in the room down the hall, heard Scotty groan, George laugh, some half-assed insults being tossed around. Joq drummed his fingers on the mattress and tried to settle his anger. He got up once he knew they were downstairs. He could hear George at the door saying something about getting ready for an away game.

"Don't do anything I wouldn't do," Scotty's voice drifted up from downstairs.

"Think that leaves my options pretty open," George scoffed.

"Exactly."

"Bye, Scotty."

"Hang on, I wanna firm promise you're gonna come see me in the off-season."

"I'll do my best." Joq could hear in George's voice he was trying to get Scotty out of there without committing to anything.

"You can bring your boy," Scotty laughed.

"Get outta here," George slammed the door.

Joq bristled. He could still hear Scotty laughing on the other side of the door before it drifted away. He felt hurt. He shoved that aside and seized on the anger. He marched down the stairs.

"What time's lunch?" George asked as he jogged up, his hand reaching out and brushing Joq's side as he passed him on the stairs.

"One."

"Cool," George went back into their room and closed the door behind him.

Joq tried to shake off the anger, the unsettled feeling. He really didn't need to broadcast any bad blood with his parents in the house.

By the third time George looked at his phone at lunch, Joq's mum said something. He'd seen her quiet surprise at the first look, the arched eyebrow at the second, and now he knew she was thinking it'd gone to straight up rude.

"Somewhere you need to be, George?" she asked and sipped her wine.

"No, sorry," he put his phone down, smiled that charming smile. "Just drinks with some old friends last night for the birthday, getting spammed with night-after gossip."

"Hmmm," she smiled at him. On anyone else, it'd be a smile enamoured with his charm. Joq's mum was immune; her smile told George he was skating on thin ice.

"Thirty-one," Joq said to head that off. "Getting old."

His dad laughed good-naturedly and started telling a story about when he was thirty-one, still coaching the national swim team. His dad could ramble, and tell a good story, and Joq smiled at him and relaxed. He glanced at George hanging on every word. George met Joq's eyes and grinned, then looked back at his dad.

"Something else happened that year," his mum said as he wound down.

"This one," his dad beamed and rubbed Joq's head like he was still a boy.

"A very pleasant surprise," she finished as she looked at Joq.

George's phone vibrated on the table. He picked it up.

"Sorry," he said as he stood. "Excuse me, I better take this."

And then he was up, strolling down the hall, his soft, "Hello," wafting back to them as he went through the door to the games room and gym.

Joq's mum didn't bother to hide her sigh. It was full of everything she thought about the situation. Joq was impressed she could do that: make one noise and communicate so much.

Joq and his parents had managed to have only one fight his entire life. But it was the kind of fight that coloured everything that came after it if they weren't careful to avoid the topic: him and George. His mum didn't like George "keeping her boy in the closet" as she put it, while his dad, an ex-champion swimmer—lots of Gold in the Commonwealth Games, never making the podium in the Olympics—always tried to get her to understand George's side. They'd had calm variations of this conversation since Joq moved in.

"If he loved you, he wouldn't do that," she'd say.

"It's not that simple, Janice," his dad would reason calmly. "You don't get the pressure, living under a microscope like that. What's private, you want to keep private. Keep as yours."

"Oh, so I don't know about the life of professional athletes, is that what you're saying?" she'd counter.

And then they'd be off: "No, I know you were there," he'd say.

"It might not have been me in the games, Jim, but physios see a lot you know," she'd retort.

And so on.

About five years ago, in the midst of this argument, she'd hit him with a knockout blow: "So, what you're saying is, if I'd been a man, you wouldn't have wanted to tell everyone about me? Show me off?"

"Of course not!" And his dad had sounded insulted, some real heat in his voice for the first time.

"Of course not, you wouldn't have told everyone?" She went on.

"Of course I would tell everyone! It's you!" He exploded.

She shot Joq a triumphant look. And Joq never forgot the flash of pity that went over his dad's face before he smiled sheepishly in an attempt to soften the blow.

The point was, now whenever the arrangement he and George shared came up, whenever George did something as blindingly stupid as take a phone call for footy stuff like now—which was a new level of stupid, even Joq could admit that—his mum looked at him and that look communicated the whole fight all over again.

Only this time, when Joq looked at her, the triumph was gone. She was angry.

"You deserve better," she said.

"Mum," he started.

"I don't want to discuss it, I'm not..." her voice petered out and she looked away. He got it. He was her only child. A happy accident when she was forty. At twelve years older than his dad, she called her husband her first happy accident and Joq her second. "Who gets together with an eighteen-year-old swimmer at thirty!" she'd laugh whenever she told the story. They'd had an idyllic life. Happy as a couple for over ten years. Happy with their only son for over twenty years after that.

Until George.

"I just mean," she looked back at him. "I think you can do better."

"You've said," he replied.

"And you're still not listening," she finished quietly as George came back in.

"Joq? Not listening?" he asked, all smiles.

"You know, Joaquin," his dad picked up a thread and ran with it, "always doing his own thing. Once, when he was a kid…"

They moved on and Joq did his best to ignore the frosty looks his mum gave George every time he looked at that damn phone.

19

I T WAS IN THE game the following weekend that things came
to a head. At least for Joq. George would continue to give off
an air of denial. But Joq knew what he saw.

There was one point in it going into the fourth. It'd been a good
game, kicks hitting chests, lots of shots on goal, high scoring. They
were down one point, but the whole building was braced with the
expectation that the home team would win it. Finn had one goal
and he'd set up some beautiful plays to create others for Lacy deep
in the pocket.

Joq was working, his team working the sections as he stood
behind them, one eye on the screen watching the game, the other
lazily drifting over the monitors every now and then.

A roar of outrage from the crowd so loud they felt it in the
room made him snap his attention back to the game. He hadn't
seen what happened, but he saw Finn on the ground, his opponent standing over him, his arms wide, mouth already moving as
he shouted denials.

Finn wasn't moving.

"Fuckin' clocked him," Simo said.

"Suspension for sure. Idiot," Cameron replied.

Joq waited for the replay. Only there was no replay because it'd happened off the ball.

"You got a view of it?"

"Yeah, here," Simo flicked to the black and white security footage.

Joq glanced back at the game screen. Finn's team mates were around him, the trainer, and then the team doctor. The footage cut to the coaches' box and Joq expected to see the concerned look in George's eyes as he waited with the rest of them to see if Finn got up.

The box was empty save for the two assistants. The shot cut to George jogging across the field. Which meant he got up right after the hit. Which meant he was already running to Finn as soon as it happened. Coaches didn't do that. George's face was a thunder cloud.

"Here," Simo said and Joq turned and watched the replay.

It was from behind, but it was pretty clear what happened—the nudge, the hip and shoulder, Finn not reacting, then the opponent clocking him right across the jaw with a fist. Finn toppled to the ground. Out cold.

Joq looked back to the game screen. George was next to Finn now, his hands careful as he tilted his face up. Joq watched as Finn's eyes blinked open and locked on George. Finn winced, but his lips curved up and he mumbled something. The trainer was trying to get to him, but it was George who slid his arms around his back and lifted him, helped him off the field.

"Damn," Simo said. "Creed really protecting his asset isn't he?"

Joq grunted. He felt Alison looking at him and very deliberately ignored it.

"Yeah, that was weird as fuck," Cameron replied and sipped on his coffee like he was watching a movie.

Joq was beginning to feel like he was watching a movie as well. But all the usual scripts for what was expected in a football game were tossed out the window. He saw George reluctantly hand Finn over to two trainers at the top of the tunnel. He said something close to Finn's ear. Finn nodded, eyes on his boots. Then George was jogging out and back up the stairs, taking them two at a time as he went back to his box.

Joq chewed on his thumb nail as he watched the rest of the game, kept an eye on the monitors. Finn was laid out in the trainer's room, but he wasn't there for long. They were moving him to meet the ambulance officers before the game had even ended.

They won it in the end, thanks to Lacy, and Joq did his best to focus on the monitors as the crowds filed out, as the team filed into the locker room, as George came in to speak to them. Only George spoke to them for less than a minute, hands waving, mouth moving rapid fire, and then he was handing his clipboard to his assistant and marching out.

Joq saw him appear on the monitor outside the locker room door, watched him walk briskly down the corridor and exit the building. He didn't need to guess where he was going, but he couldn't quite believe it.

Joq waited up, an anxious feeling swirling around in his gut, and thought about what to say. Ask how Finn was, obviously. Ask why George went to him on the field. Maybe suggest George think about how that might fucking look to the whole world.

Then again, he knew George would shrug that off with the same argument Joq had been giving him for years—*no one's gonna think that 'cos no one wants to believe something like that is going on in this sport.*

True enough.

But by the time it was two in the morning, Joq conceded George probably wasn't going to come home. He was spending the night with Finn in the hospital. And that made him want to ask the question he really wanted to ask: did George think about how all of this made *him* feel?

But he'd shot himself in the foot with that one years ago when he got George to concede to an open relationship. George was a one man kinda guy. And that was something Joq really tried not to think about anymore. It used to make him feel good, really good. Now it terrified him.

His thumb nail was bitten to the skin and bleeding by the time he went to bed. He couldn't sleep, all he could do was listen to these thoughts as they travelled across his brain on repeat as he waited for George to come home.

Joq was making his takeaway coffee and slapping his lanyard out of the way when he heard George come in the next morning. He hadn't slept, and he'd gone from fearful about what this all meant to furious.

"Hey," George breathed out as he came into the kitchen.

"Hey," Joq replied and looked over at him. George gave him a wan smile, his eyes bloodshot and flanked with shadows, his expression apologetic.

"I gotta go to work," Joq said instead of anything and everything else.

"He's gonna be alright," George said.

Joq went past him and did his best to bite his tongue, but a bitter, mumbled thought managed to come out: "Yeah, I don't give a shit."

"What?" George asked. He sounded genuinely surprised. The asshole.

"Seriously?" Joq spun back to him. "Since when does a coach sit at a player's bedside all night? How do you think that looks?"

"I don't give a shit how it looks," George said.

"Well maybe you should," Joq spat. "Oh and by the way, the phone is a thing."

"You knew where I was," George said and had the audacity to sound incredulous. "I don't get why you're so mad."

Joq didn't know how to explain why he was so mad without saying something that would put ideas in George's head. Ideas Joq was afraid would lead George straight to Finn.

"Just, I'm gonna be late," he shook his head. Then he met George's bewildered expression. "Just, twelve years is not nothing, you know."

George sucked in a breath like he couldn't believe what Joq was saying.

"I know," George said. "But what's that got to do with anything?"

It was Joq's turn to give him an incredulous look. "A phone call. I think it means I deserve a phone call if you're not coming home."

Well, that was a tiny part of it.

George nodded, chastised. "You're right, I'm sorry. I was just, he was—

"It's fine!" Joq cut him off.

George stopped, startled.

"It's fine. I gotta go. See you tonight."

Joq was turning and heading for the door, but he heard George calling after him just fine.

"Okay, but I might not be here, but I'll call..."

Joq slammed the door on his way out.

Fuck.

F INN HAD A CONCUSSION and wouldn't travel with the team that
weekend to Queensland.

"He's pretty down about it, was gonna make his own way back after
going home, seeing his family, his dog..." George trailed off. Probably
because Joq was not doing a great job of keeping the *'I don't give
a flying fuck!'* look off his face whenever George mentioned Finn's
condition.

Joq was in the living room, George was in the hall checking his
pockets, his bag at his feet, ready to go meet the team and catch their
flight.

"I'll call when I get to the hotel," George said.

"Okay," Joq replied. He wasn't going to offer to take him to the
airport. They'd been tiptoeing around each other all week. Breaking
routine without saying why seemed like a much safer option than
sitting in the car together at the moment.

"Got any plans?" George asked.

Joq saw he was trying, saw he'd taken that remark about twelve years
to heart. Joq decided that wasn't nothing.

"Mum's birthday," Joq said.

"Oh, shit. Well, here, let me," George was reaching for his wallet.

Joq held up his hand with a smile. "I already got it. Your name's on the card."

"Shit, thanks, babe," George smiled. "Sorry, been a bit distracted—

"It's fine," Joq said and got up. "Good luck. Shouldn't be too hard to take Brisbane, yeah?"

George slid his arms around Joq's waist and tugged him in once Joq was in front of him.

"Don't jinx it," he said into the crook of Joq's shoulder and neck.

Joq huffed a laugh, turned his head. George met him with a firm kiss.

"Sorry, I just can't be assed giving you a lift," Joq lied.

He knew George knew it was a lie and appreciated the way he nodded, too eagerly. "All good, you deserve a night off."

Joq smiled and leaned in for another kiss. George met him, but he pulled back first and stepped away, shouldered his bag.

"Call you when I get there," he said again.

"Yep," Joq shoved his hands in his pockets.

George nodded, turned and let the door fall shut quietly behind him as he left.

"Yep," Joq breathed out again to no one.

The team did take Brisbane, and Joq smiled when he thought about how they did it without Finn. He caught that thought and told himself to stop it. Having a hate-on for the kid wasn't going to help. And besides, Finn was just too young to stay mad at. Poor kid was probably going through his first real crush.

He was back training with the team, taking it easy under concussion protocol, but back in the room, as Joq could see in high definition in that moment while he went through the job with Cameron's replacement. Sue. An older woman, ex-navy, she wanted something less demanding so she could "Spend time with the grandkids."

Joq liked the military air she gave off and the fact she detested the team. It made him laugh. She was a die-hard supporter of their biggest rival, but she said she could remain professional about it. This also made him laugh.

"I'm sure," he said and ran through the monitors, explained the importance of ensuring all cameras were recording at all times in case something happened and management or the authorities needed it.

"Of course," Sue said. She said it like, *'No shit.'*

Joq suppressed his smile and leaned back, folded his arms over his chest and left her to it. Simo was helpfully pointing things out while Sue looked at him like she couldn't quite believe he was real; his liquorice strap hanging out of his mouth, his skinny body taking up more space than it reasonably should as he gestured and spoke around his teeth caked with black candy.

"Ugh, Creed," Sue said as George appeared on the monitors in the locker room.

"Creed's the fucking shit!" Simo said.

"Over-rated."

Simo spluttered. "Over-rated! Did you see the 2016 Grand Final? That was all him, baby. All him."

Sue snorted. "You won that by default. They lost, you didn't win-it, win-it."

"Oh my God," Simo started and Joq tuned them out. He'd heard this argument. And he hated to concede that, yeah, they kind of had taken full advantage of the opposition completely choking on the big stage. Still, George had played the game of his life, kicking seven beautiful goals. Joq could still see the image of him in his mind when he jogged up and took the Norm Smith for best player on ground—his brown hair long and wavy in the breeze, his modest smile—he'd deserved it regardless of whatever else happened in that game. He'd been on fire, a true legend coming of age.

He was on the monitor now, moving around his players, speaking to each one individually, his notes forgotten by his side.

Joq tensed as he watched him approach Finn in front of his stall. Finn had been having a friendly shoving match with Lacy, but he straightened as George came over. Lacy got up, flicked Finn in the head with his towel; Finn batted it away with a laugh, but George said something to Lacy which had him raising his hands and then clearly apologising to Finn.

Other than that, the interaction between George and Finn seemed carefully professional. Too careful? Joq rubbed his jaw as he watched. No, he focused on Finn, on his Bambi fucking eyes looking up at George, the hint of a questioning smile on his face while George spoke. No, it was George who was all business, his face blank as he said something more and then walked off. Finn looked hurt as he watched George's back.

Joq swallowed. Well, alright then. Alright.

That night when George came home and found Joq in his office and kissed him hello, Joq felt something sincere in it, something like before.

"Hi," he said as he smiled up at him.

"Wanna go out for dinner?" George asked.

"Yeah, sounds good. Just gotta finish some tax stuff."

"Take your time," George said as he went out, smiled over his shoulder.

And, alright then. Joq felt like he could breathe again. This was normal. This was good.

21

S O, THINGS AT HOME were good. Things at work were good. Sue and Alison got along well, seemed to find mutual ground in mocking Simo, which made Simo preen like he was being flirted with. Cameron's missus had the baby and everyone was doing well. Joq sent them a bouquet and a teddy with a surveillance camera in it from the crew. Cameron sent a laughing emoji to the group chat.

It was good. It was his life again. Joq relaxed enough to start looking seriously through his messages, his apps, to start planning a decent hook-up when George headed to South Australia that weekend.

The team had won another game the day before against a struggling inner city team, but a win was a win and everyone seemed well going into post-game training that Monday morning as far as Joq could see. Well, everyone except Finn. He'd played like shit on the weekend and Joq hadn't missed the talking heads diagnosing him as *"Rattled. Kid's rattled. He needs to get over it. He's playing with the big boys now, he needs to learn to shake it off."* Joq glanced at him in the locker room, the slump of his shoulders where he was sitting in front of his stall, his face hidden by his hair. It was one game, it was nothing.

Joq was on shift with Alison and Simo, watching the players still on the field, some of them in the locker room with Finn, some guys coming and going from the trainer's, getting physio, George stepping into his office.

He was preparing to swap out the current data files for new ones, put these ones in storage. He barely paid any attention when he saw Finn following the team doctor to one of the rooms. He noticed Finn sitting on one of the beds in an idle way, the doctor shining a light in both eyes, asking him questions. Finn flinched.

Joq paused from what he was doing and watched. Finn shook his head, his smile strained. The doctor tilted his head to the side, studied Finn before him; then he turned and went out. Finn slumped and held his head in his hands.

Joq really felt bad for him then. He might actually have post-concussion syndrome, which could end his season. That empathy fled when he saw George come into the room. Finn didn't even look up.

Joq stilled. He could hear Simo talking and Alison murmuring something back in a distant way—his eyes were fixed on George going over to Finn, on his long fingers gently sliding under Finn's chin and lifting his head, on the way Finn's eyes met George's, on the sheen there. Joq felt like he must've been imagining it as he watched George lean forward and press his lips against Finn's. Finn's lips parted and he kissed back, suddenly very animated, very alive. He watched in shocked silence as George pulled away and said something against Finn's lips before stepping back, letting him go. Finn's lips were parted, his chest rising and falling, his eyes wide on George.

"What. The. Fuck," Simo said, snapping Joq back to the room.

Joq couldn't tear his eyes away as he watched Finn start to smile, as George smiled back; he was smiling at Finn like no one else existed except the kid in front of him. The doctor came back in and George said something to him and left the room.

"Did that just..." Alison said.

"We've all signed NDAs," Joq heard himself say.

"No, but, what the fuck, what the actual fuck?" Simo asked.

"Can you get that?" Joq asked him.

"Yeah? What? You mean like, take the file out?"

"Yes," Joq said firmly.

"Yeah, but."

"Get the file," Alison cut in. "Then erase it. Yeah?" She turned to Joq.

He nodded. "Yes."

"What the fuck," Simo said under his breath but did as he was told. He kept repeating himself, but eventually turned to Joq. "Erased it."

"Good," Joq nodded. "We've all signed NDAs," he said again.

"Yeah, don't reckon that's the problem, boss," Simo said.

Joq looked at him. "You got a problem with that?"

Simo raised his palms. "Hey, I ain't got no problem with dudes banging other dudes, but I mean. He's the *coach*."

Joq cleared his throat, and he reckoned he deserved an Oscar for what came out of his mouth next, for his neutral expression: "And I think it's none of our business. Forget about it. Let's move on. Alison, can you finish downloading the old files? Simo, show her how to do back up and storage. I'll be back."

And he got the hell out of there.

Alison caught him before he'd even made it out of the break room.

"Hey," she called.

Joq stopped, took a deep breath and turned to her, his face carefully blank. "All good?"

"Yeah, fine. But are you alright?"

Joq jerked his head. "All good. Just gotta. Got some things..."

"That was fucked up," she said.

Joq shook his head. "It's not what it looks like. We're, you know, open."

"Oh," she said, realisation dawning in her eyes. But then she narrowed them. "You're open like that though?"

"Like what?" He did not want to have this conversation but he seemed to have lost his ability to get out of it.

"Like, that wasn't a couple of people who are just fucking," she said. The words were so matter of fact it made Joq wince.

"It's fine," he said again and tried to smile.

She gave him a pitying look.

"Get those files to storage. I'll be back," he turned and headed out the door before she could say anything else.

Joq sat outside by the pool that night, drinking a soda water. He watched the filter bubble, and listened to the distant hum of traffic.

George found him out there.

"Hey, there you are," he said. He was smiling. Joq could hear it in his voice.

"Hey," Joq replied but didn't look at him.

He wanted to confront him, but he wanted to see if George would tell him something had started first.

"You alright?"

"Yeah, course," Joq said, his eyes still fixed on the pool. He could hear George breathing. He waited.

"Alright, well, I'm gonna cook, you want anything in particular?"

Joq almost laughed. Everything felt surreal.

"You only know how to make stir-fry," he replied.

George laughed. "I can always order something."

Joq sipped his water. "Stir-fry's fine."

"Cool, give me thirty, just gonna shower," George said and Joq listened as he went back inside.

22

J OQ ALMOST DIDN'T WATCH the away game that weekend. It would've been a first, but Finn wouldn't be there—he was still suffering minor concussion symptoms, though he wasn't officially post-concussion syndrome yet—and decided he could do it.

He forgot playing or not, Finn would be there. Finn would be there sitting on the bench in his suit looking handsome and relaxed, chatting with the guys like they'd been friends forever, watching the game with serious focus, and exchanging words with George around mutual smiles between quarters.

Before the start of the third, Joq looked on with mute horror as George clapped Finn on the shoulder and leaned in close to say something against his ear. Finn was still laughing as he tucked his hands into his pockets, eyes on the ground as he went back over to the bench.

Joq clenched his jaw and decided he might as well accept it. They were going to fuck, if they hadn't already. It didn't mean him and George were going to break up.

And, for some bizarre reason, that thought drew him up short. The action continued on the screen but he wasn't watching anymore. Over the last couple of months, he hadn't seriously considered that possibility. He'd thought... George would have a fling with someone he momentarily liked more than he liked Joq. He wouldn't fucking leave him... would he?

In another almost first, Joq almost let George's facetime call ring out. He was lying in their bed, laptop open, the smile-grimace of George's picture looking up at him as the call came in later that night.

It was tradition: George always face-timed after the game, after dinner, after drinks. Joq was always the last thing he did on the road on game day. It was their thing.

And it was that thought that made him pick up.

"Hey," George said.

"Hi," Joq replied.

"How's it going?" George asked; his breathing was shallow, his smile too big.

"Good," Joq answered slowly. "You? Good game."

That got a snort from George. "You gettin' a funny sense of humour on me this season, Joaquin?"

All the hairs on Joq's body stood up. Not 'babe.' Not even 'Joq.' 'Joaquin.'

But the thing about a long-term relationship was all the words were set down. It was like a speech given a thousand times; it came even through the nerves.

"Sorry, another loss?"

"You didn't see?"

"No. Well, not all of it, had some shit to do."

"Ahh," George gave him a knowing look. "We lost."

"I had to help my parents move some furniture," Joq heard how defensive he sounded.

George could too judging by the way he sat back, glanced away from the camera.

"Nothing doing after?" George looked back and smiled.

It was wrong, an imitation of their usual conversations.

"When?" Joq asked. He shook his head. "So, loss?"

George sighed and told him about the game. It felt almost normal by the time George finished.

"Sucks, babe," Joq said.

George glanced away from the camera again. "I better go."

"Oh, okay."

"Gotta eat. I'll see you tomorrow."

"Okay, text me the time."

"Yeah, okay. Night," and then he was gone.

Joq leaned back on his pillow. He stared at his screensaver—another photo of George, only Joq was in this one as well, a selfie taken on the beach in Koh Samui their first summer after Joq moved in. Joq loved that photo—they were so young, everything felt simple and clean, their beaming faces encapsulating the joy at having found each other.

"*He gone?*" Joq heard from the laptop. It was in the background, but it was Finn. Clear as a bell.

"*Yeah,*" he heard George breath out.

George must've minimised the chat window but left the laptop open. He did that, he said, so he could just open it and call again before he left the room.

"*C'mere,*" George's voice was low. He was nervous.

Joq flushed, his skin prickling with the situation. He should shut his laptop. He should walk away. He didn't need to hear this.

But Joq could see it too if he wanted. He'd told George a thousand times to put a band-aid or blue-tack over his camera. George always snorted, 'Whose gonna wanna watch me staring at my screen?'

Right now, Joq wanted very much to see what George was about to do on his screen. He slid his laptop closer and hacked the camera. The image that accosted him almost made him gasp. He hit the mute button.

Finn was standing over George in nothing but loose sweats, chest bare, his legs shifting like he was rolling his feet on the carpet. George was sitting on the edge of the bed, his hands reaching out to slide up the side of Finn's thighs.

"*What do you want?*" George asked shakily, but sure too; it was a genuine question.

Finn breathed out above him, equally shaky. "*What do you want?*" He placed his hands on George's shoulders tentatively.

George arched up and Finn bent to meet him.

Joq watched them kiss. It was so careful—their lips barely brushing, the sound of their breathing obscenely loud. It was George who added the hint of tongue.

Joq's own breathing had grown loud in his ears as he watched them feel the other out and find the same overwhelming desire, held back by some shyness that said more about what Joq was witnessing than anything else.

This was their first time.

Finn spoke against George's lips. "*I want to suck you off.*"

George groaned and deepened the kiss.

Finn met him, panting. He broke the kiss and searched George's eyes then surged back in for more. He pulled away again and they moved as one to get Finn to his knees between George's spread thighs—Finn slunk down while George wrapped a big palm around his nape.

Finn's breathing was laboured as he looked at George's dick—hard and thick as it strained against the fabric.

"*The idea is to suck it*," George said.

"*George*," Finn whined, but he cracked up and dropped his head on George's abdomen. His body shook as he laughed, and Joq watched George smiling down at him, the hand on Finn's nape tugging his hair.

Finn got himself under control, sat back and flicked his eyes up.

"*I want...*" Finn trailed off.

"*Whatever you want*," George replied, heartbreakingly sincere, and Joq realised he'd never heard him sound like that. He was the one about to get his dick sucked, but he sounded like he was completely at the kid's mercy.

Finn leaned forward and rested his head on George's thigh, let out a harsh breath. George's hand went into his hair as he leaned down to press a kiss to the top of his head, his voice a murmur. "*You want to stop, you tell me*."

Finn's head jerked up. "*I don't want to stop*."

George kissed him and slid Finn's hand to his dick.

Joq watched as Finn gripped him through the material. He rubbed, uncoordinated, and George tilted Finn's head back with the hand in his hair, seizing his mouth in a kiss like he couldn't stop himself. Finn melted into it, his body going lax at the assault.

It was George who slid his hand down and under Finn's, got his dick out and brought Finn's hand back.

Finn stroked and leaned forward. Joq could hear his breathing, loud through the speakers as he gusted a breath over George's erection. George's breathing was just as loud, and Joq's eyes snagged on things—the tiny creases of skin in George's lower abdomen, the steel quality of his dick, the brown of Finn's fingers wrapped around his shaft.

Joq felt it in his own dick when Finn licked the head. He couldn't stop himself if he tried—he was reaching down, squeezing his dick as he watched the most intimate porn he'd ever seen.

Finn was sucking the head into his mouth, air coming out of his nose harshly. George gripped and released his hair as he rocked his hips up, his own breathing so laboured it was devastatingly loud through the speakers.

Finn took his time, whether from inexperience or reverence, Joq had no idea, but he was mesmerised as he watched the kid slide down, slide off, lick around the head before sucking George back down like he was driven by need and not thought. George's eyes were fixed on him and Joq could see he was doing his best not to buck into Finn's mouth.

But then Finn sank all the way down, and Joq had to squeeze his dick to stop from coming at the guttural sound George made, his hips driving in without his control. Joq thought Finn would pull off, but he did it again—slid up until the tip was in his mouth, his eyes flicking up to George's before he sank down again.

"*Fuck, baby. Finn,*" George panted and rocked his hips up. "*Can I fuck your mouth?*"

Finn pulled up and off. His voice was a husk: "*Yeah. Please.*"

George groaned and gripped him by the hair, his movements clumsy as he drove into Finn's panting mouth.

Jesus, Joq thought as he stroked himself in time to George's thrusts—slow but deep, his breathing the same measured pace. Joq knew it was wrong, he knew it was wrong on so many levels, but he couldn't stop himself.

Tears pooled in Finn's blue eyes, the whites turning soft red. He whined around George's cock and ran his hands up and down George's muscled thighs, then up his chest under his shirt. His eyes fixed on George's above him as he took that cock like he didn't want to be anywhere else.

George's hips sped up. "*You can swallow?*"

Finn moaned around the onslaught on his mouth, his throat.

"*Oh, God. You can swallow,*" George bit out before he was slamming in, his hips jerking in deep as he came.

Finn groaned around him, and Joq felt himself start to come as he watched that throat swallowing, those eyes streaming with tears, never closing, never leaving George's.

Joq was panting, his hand covered in come and snug around his softening dick.

George slid his dick out of Finn's mouth and yanked him into his lap, kissed him so passionately, Joq thought you'd never guess the man had just come.

Finn was a mess—whining, grinding, kissing George back like he'd lost complete control of himself. It was a scene alright—that big, athletic body cradled in George's lap, muscles flexing, straining to get closer as he ran his hands under George's shirt and tugged until George pulled away to tear it off.

Once George's head popped free, he took Finn's mouth in a brutal kiss before lifting him and shoving him onto his back so they were stretched out on the end of the bed.

George leaned up on his elbow, his breathing harsh; but a small smile started at the corner of his lips. He ran his hand roughly over Finn's trembling body. "*Geeze, Finny, you wanting somethin'?*"

"*George,*" Finn whined, his body shaking with laughter. "*Please.*"

"*I dunno,*" George ran his hand down and cupped Finn's dick. "*I don't reckon you need me, reckon you got it covered.*"

Finn started thrusting into his hand and giggling at the same time so the whole action was ungainly, yet strangely sexy—the two of them stretched out, huffing breaths of laughter as they watched each other.

Joq felt his dick pulse when George broke the moment and slid down between Finn's legs, tugged his pants off and pushed his thighs open.

Finn was shaking, his uncut dick hard and straining against his abs, his hands sinking into George's thick hair to hold on.

George brought his head up and sucked Finn down in one go, tip to root and back again; slow, practiced, and Joq knew he was good at that, but this was something else—this was reverent. George's finger rubbed Finn's perineum in a slow drag in time with his mouth.

Finn arched off the bed when George pulled off. "*No, please,*" he gasped.

And Joq couldn't quite believe what he was seeing when he realised what George was doing. One hand on Finn's dick, stroking slowly; he brought his mouth down and started to lick at Finn's hole. George never ate ass. Never. He fucking well was now—his tongue pushing in until he was fucking Finn in time with the hand on the kid's dick.

Joq squeezed his own dick. Finn was rocking his hips down, trying to get more, pushing his hips up, trying to get more, and his voice was weak as he begged. "*Please, please. George, please...*"

George brought in a finger and wedged it alongside his tongue. He fucked Finn like that, slow and deep, his hand and mouth never speeding up.

Joq watched with fascination when Finn's body went taut and he arched, his eyes wide on the ceiling. George got his mouth back on his dick and sucked him down as he shoved in with two fingers and fucked him through his orgasm.

Jesus, Joq could record this and make a small fortune in porn. Pity their faces were clear as day. He watched as Finn came and came and George never wavered, sucking him off, fucking him with his fingers steadily. By the time Finn sagged into the mattress, Joq was rock hard again.

George let Finn go and slid up the bed, tucking his body next to Finn's. His hand stroked his chest, played with his nipples.

Finn cracked his eyes open. He was panting, he was smiling. George smiled down at him.

"*Fuck*," Finn breathed out. "*What was that?*"

"*An orgasm?*" George grinned.

Finn huffed a laugh. He moved his head and George was meeting him like he read the play before it even started.

Joq felt like they kissed for an inordinately long time. Long, slow kisses; kisses that weren't going anywhere; kisses that were just for the pleasure of feeling the other person that way, being close like that. He watched them as they moved together—George's hand never ceased in its caress all over Finn's chest and abs; Finn's hands stroking over George's body in the same soft way.

It was Finn who pulled back. "*Ten out of ten, will fuck again.*"

George laughed down at him. "*We haven't fucked yet.*"

"*But we will?*" Finn asked, he smiled playfully and his eyes shone.

George brought his hand up and stroked his fingers down Finn's cheek so gently it made Joq ache.

"*We will.*"

"*Just fuck?*"

George frowned.

"*Just fucking,*" he said after a moment.

Finn searched George's eyes and George let him do it. The way they were looking at each other made Joq think they'd discussed this before.

Eventually, Finn nodded. "*Okay.*"

George rolled away and got up. He was off camera now and Joq watched as Finn squeezed his eyes closed.

"*Order something, no junk,*" George said.

"*Okay,*" Finn replied, eyes still closed.

"*Then meet me in the shower.*"

Finn's eyes flicked open and he was looking over to George; Joq couldn't see George, but he did not miss the sunshine smile breaking over Finn's face.

Joq lay there, his dick still hard, his eyes on the ceiling, the laptop open, the sound of the shower behind a closed door in that hotel room tinny through his speakers.

"*Just fucking,*" George had said. Had said it firmly too.

That had not been just fucking. Denial was Joq's best friend here, but he wasn't fucking stupid; he knew what he'd just seen. He'd had a lot of hook-ups, friendly ones, intimate ones. He'd never done anything like that. Not even with George.

He heard the shower door open, and rolled his head to the side to watch. George was coming out, towel around his waist, telling Finn he'd get the room service. Finn didn't emerge.

The thing Joq had to count on, he thought as he watched George slick his wet hair back from his face and lean down to pick up his sweats, was George's denial. *Just fucking.*

Joq didn't know why he kept watching after that. They weren't doing anything outwardly untoward. Sitting on the bed together near the headboard, George was leaning back and eating with one hand, the other running up and down Finn's back; Finn was sitting forward, eating one handed as well, his other hand running up the inseam of George's pants.

They were watching a replay of a game. Joq had to concede Finn had a good head for it after about twenty minutes.

"*He's using Besson wrong,*" Finn was saying. "*Put him in the mid-field, he's fast and he's got skills. If they knock out to him from the centre bounce, he'll take it and get it to the pocket every time.*"

"*Hmmm,*" George said. "*Whose he gonna put in the forward pocket though?*"

"*Carr,*" Finn said like it was obvious.

George snorted. Finn looked over his shoulder at him. "*It's true. He can take a beauty of a mark if you play him right. And he's not scared to jump for them. All of them.*"

"*He's out of shape.*"

"*Exactly. So why play him in the mid-field? He's got mad fucking skills though, don't need to be fit for that.*"

"*Hmmm,*" George said and squeezed Finn's shoulder before resuming the caress. Joq knew that meant George agreed with the assessment, was taking it in and applying it to his own thinking.

They went on like that for the whole game. The conversation made Joq as uncomfortable as the swapped blowjobs had.

When Setter, an ex-player recently made head coach after doing years as an assistant must've come on screen, Finn said, "*Wow, Setter's really let himself go.*"

George snorted. "*Benefit of coaching and not playing.*"

"*Yeah?*" Finn shot him a cheeky smile over his shoulder. "*You planning to?*"

"*I dunno,*" George ran his hand down Finn's back and smiled. "*I do like pies.*"

Finn scoffed.

George brought his hand to Finn's side and started tickling him. "*Will you still like me if I tub out?*"

Finn wriggled away, laughing.

"*You won't?*" George grabbed him around the waist.

"*I might,*" Finn said, breathless with laughter.

"*Might?*" George really laid into him then—got both hands into his sides and Finn tried to get away, choking on his laughter.

"*Alright, alright, I'll still like your fat ass.*"

"*I'll give you a fat ass...*"

Joq felt like he was having an outer body experience as he watched them wrestling, then kissing; or trying to around their laughter.

A roar from the TV made them look up as one.

"*See?*" Finn said. "*I told you.*"

"*Yeah, alright,*" George said and kissed Finn's Adam's apple.

"*No, seriously, watch the replay. I'm tellin' you, he needs to play Carr in the pocket.*"

George looked up again, and judging by the matching looks of concentration on their faces, they were watching a replay of the mark, then a replay of the goal. Joq didn't need to see it to know it; Finn had a point, Carr could take a hell of a mark, and he was a good kick.

George grunted.

"*What? He's good*," Finn said, eyes still on the screen. "*I'm telling you, forward pocket.*"

Joq could hear enough to know they were replaying it from another angle.

"*See?*" Finn said. "*Fuckin' beauty. Man, he looks good. Still.*"

"*He's alright*," George said and rolled up to sit, dragging Finn with him. "*I met his girlfriend at the Brownlow's last year—she's nicer than him.*"

Finn laughed. They'd resumed the same position—George's hand on Finn's back, Finn sitting forward to watch the game as he held George's inner thigh.

"*Real smooth, old man,*" Finn said.

"*What?*" George raised both eyebrows.

Finn glanced back at him and Joq watched as George's pretence slipped—smiling like he'd been caught, like he wanted to get caught.

"*I'm just saying,*" George went on, "*she's a nice lady.*"

"*Oh, that's all you're saying is it?*" Finn's voice had taken on the same playful edge as George's, like he was also trying to keep up the façade for the fun of it.

"*Yes, and they seem very happy.*"

Finn giggled. "*Okay, I'll stop myself from trying to get in on that then.*"

"*Damn right you will,*" George tickled his side again and Joq felt like he'd had just about enough of watching this. It'd gone from surreal to uncomfortable.

George and Finn settled, watched the game, their hands wandering aimlessly.

Joq was getting sleepy and he didn't think he was going to learn anything more about where his boyfriend's head was at than he already had.

He was wrong.

Joq was about to slam the laptop shut when he noticed Finn's hand inching closer to George's dick. It was subtle, the way he was drifting his fingers higher, then dragging them down, his eyes still on the TV. George cocked his leg out, an invitation for more, and ran his own hand lower down Finn's back. Joq couldn't see from this angle, but he did see the way Finn sat forward, giving George more room to stroke under his pants, tease his ass.

Joq rolled to the side and cradled his head in his hand, suddenly very awake.

Finn's hand made another few passes, just skimming the fabric at the base of George's hardening dick. George's bicep flexed like he was stroking lower, his breathing rough. Finn brought his hand up and rubbed it over George's dick, eyes forward, but his focus was on that hand as he stroked up, then down, squeezed. George made a low sound and Finn glanced back at him.

Joq couldn't make out either of their expressions with the back of Finn's head obscuring his view, but he could hear it when they started to kiss. The slick sound of mouths moving together slowly, increasing in time with the hand he could see working George over, George's arm moving like he was shifting his hand for better access.

They were going to fuck. Joq knew it then and his conscience gave a valiant whisper to turn it off. Instead, he let his hand drift down so he could grip himself. He was awash with jealousy, yet he was too turned on to care.

It was George who brought both arms up, wrapped them around Finn and tugged him into his lap, their kisses never stopping, not even when George wrestled Finn's pants off, pulled him snug into his chest with a slap of skin on skin.

He did break away to click the TV off with the remote, then lean down for his bag beside the bed. Finn stroked his chest, kissed up his throat, worshipped George's body while he ground his hips forward on George's abs. George came back and wrapped one big arm around Finn's back, tossed a bottle of lube and a string of condoms at his hip.

So, it was planned. Joq didn't stop jerking off as that realisation hit him. No, he kept working his cock as he watched George give Finn the condoms, grab the lube and pour some into his hand, then reach around and breach Finn with two fingers at once, cradling Finn as he arched and gasped.

It was an explicit view in a way, Joq thought—Finn's broad shoulders, tapered waist and firm ass; the back of his head, the mess of his hair; the long planes of his back obscuring all but the view of George's fingers as they drove into his ass and Finn rocked back to meet them. Joq heard the rip of the foil, and recognised the movement of Finn's hands as him rolling it down George's length.

He held his own dick as it throbbed in his palm, held his breath too as he waited for it.

George pulled his fingers out and gripped Finn's hip with one hand, the other one sliding up to hold his nape. He lifted him and Joq could see Finn holding George's cock, angling it until he was hovering over the tip before rubbing it gently against his entrance. George pushed him down and thrust up at the same time. Finn's gasp was lost as George used his other hand to tug him into a kiss.

George held him steady as he fucked into him. He built a steady rhythm with his feet planted on the mattress. Then he relaxed his grip on Finn's hip, on his head. Finn arched and rode him, met George's cock with a roll of his hips, rolled his head back and gasped.

"*Look at you,*" George breathed out. "*Fuck, look at you.*"

Finn keened.

"Jesus," Joq said under his breath as he watched.

George looked over his shoulder and Joq froze. For a second he thought George had heard him, seen him; but then he realised he was looking at the mirror, looking at the picture he and Finn made together. The same picture Joq was seeing—Finn impaled on George's big cock, George thrusting up into him, Finn riding him with his powerful thighs, his head thrown back.

George kissed up his neck, spoke into his ear. "*You have to see. Have to see how good you look.*"

Finn gasped and slammed himself down on George's cock. George groaned but tightened his hold, stilled him.

"*Turn around,*" George said against his ear.

Finn tried to move his hips, but George didn't let him. Finn turned his head to kiss him desperately. George kissed him back but then pulled away.

"*Turn around, baby. Hands and knees,*" he said and pulled out.

Finn groaned but moved when George moved him. He was a sight—his hair still drying and now prickling with sweat and sticking up everywhere, his face flushed, his eyes widening as they landed on himself—on where Joq was watching.

George came up on his knees behind him and ran his broad palms over Finn's back. He left one hand on his shoulder. The other one dragged down to grip his hip to hold him still. He looked up and met Finn's eyes in the mirror.

Finn's lips parted.

George pushed in, his eyes never leaving Finn's as he slid inside. He drove his hips forward until he was flush against Finn's ass. Then he paused.

Joq had never thought of George as a particularly dominating lover. He'd always been good in bed, solid, but this was another side of him. He watched as George paused, held Finn still, held eye contact, and Finn watched him back, suspended, like they were exchanging something.

"*Look at yourself while I fuck you*," George said.

Joq gasped at that. So did Finn. And Joq thought, case in point—who was this man?

Finn's eyes focused on himself in the mirror. The position made it seem like he was looking right at Joq. He was blushing, shy. George drew back and then pushed in, rocking Finn forward. Finn's eyes slipped closed as if he couldn't watch.

George stopped and plastered himself over Finn's back. He wrapped his arm around his chest and hoisted him up.

And wow. Now Joq was getting an absolute eyeful. Finn's abs were taut as George pulled him back against his chest, his dick hard and straining up, George's cock lodged deep in his ass. Finn's chest heaved as he tried to breathe. George had a tight hold on him, powerful thighs bracketing him as his arm held him upright.

George gently brushed Finn's hair aside with his nose, kissed the skin below his ear and whispered, "*You look so good like this, so good*," he pressed another kiss to his cheek, "*Look*."

Finn whimpered, an incongruous sound from that powerful body, but did as he was told. He glanced up and his lips parted as he took in the scene.

George ran a hand up Finn's chest, rested it over his heart. Finn made a little broken sound. George kissed his ear and whispered something Joq couldn't hear.

Then he started to fuck him again. He kissed his throat, his shoulder, didn't pull his dick out too far, fucked him deep and close. His eyes flicked up to meet Finn's in the mirror. He slid a hand to Finn's dick and started to jerk him off.

Joq could see the orgasm before it happened in the way Finn went tense in George's arms, in the widening of his eyes, in the way George sped up like he knew it too. Watching him come from this position was better than any pornography Joq had ever seen. Finn let it crash into him, like he was sure George would hold him together when he did. And George did, fucking him through it, kissing his neck, eyes still on him, voice muffled in Finn's skin as he told him how good he looked, how perfect he was, how lucky George was to be with him like this.

Finn slumped in George's arms.

Joq was close to the edge himself when George went to pull out.

Finn brought his hand back to hold him in.

George groaned, buried his face in the crook of Finn's shoulder and neck.

Finn brought his other hand up and held George's head, kissed his hair, whispered something Joq couldn't make out.

It was a reversal: Finn looked strong as George fucked into him erratically. Finn took it and held him close, his own body shaking minutely at the pounding, but solid too, there for it.

George came with a groan and a series of deep thrusts like he was trying to bury himself inside Finn. Finn held him, took all of it.

"Fuck," Joq said as he came to the sight.

He rolled onto his back and left his hand where it was, covered in his second lot of come. He needed to get up and change his boxers. He could hear George and Finn kissing. He made out the sound of sheets rustling, a tap running in the distance, the shift of a body getting into bed, more kissing.

Between one breath and the next, Joq drifted off.

When he woke, it was just getting light. He couldn't work out why he'd woken up. He could hear something, like a movie. He rolled his head to the side and the night before crashed over him as he looked at the dim hotel room. It was still too dark there to make out much, but he could hear it well enough—the sound of skin slapping on skin, panting breaths, a guttural moan, kisses that sounded desperate and wet.

Joq groaned, rolled over, and slammed his laptop shut.

23

LATER THAT AFTERNOON, JOQ got a text from George saying he was going back to the club with the team, no need for an airport pick-up.

Joq didn't reply.

He felt shaky. He felt like he'd seen a lot he shouldn't have. He felt bad about that. But he also had a sick kind of curiosity brewing in him, a self-righteous anger. He wanted to confront George about it. He wanted to wait and see if George would tell him first.

If it was just a hook-up, then he should tell Joq about it. That was the rule.

George still wasn't home by midnight. Joq went to bed. He heard George come in shortly after.

As George slipped in beside him, Joq rolled over.

"Sorry," George whispered. "Go back to sleep."

Joq slid his hand over George's stomach, slid lower. George stopped him.

"Not tonight, go back to sleep," he said again, then removed Joq's hand, rolled over and breathed in a way that said he wasn't sleeping either.

Joq rolled over and faced the other side of the room, wide awake. He didn't remember falling asleep.

When Joq came home from work the following evening, George was sitting in the living room. He stood when Joq came in.

"Hey," Joq said.

"Hey," George sounded nervous. "Can we talk?"

Joq's heart sped up. "Yeah, course."

"Okay," George sat back down.

Joq took his shoes off and came into the living room. His stomach was flipping over and his mouth was dry.

"What's up?" he asked as casually as he could and sat in the armchair.

George sat forward, clasped his hands, fixed his eyes on his hands.

Oh, God, Joq thought, he was going to break up with him.

"I... I decided to..." George cleared his throat.

Joq swallowed. Tried to prepare for it.

"We're open," George said, matter of fact, and glanced up. "So, I fucked around."

Joq nodded his head slowly. "Okay," he said and swallowed. "Is this your attempt at foreplay?" He tried for the joke and felt it land flat.

George's face contorted like the idea revolted him. "No. Definitely, no," he shook his head. "I don't want to... like you do. If that's okay," he rushed on at the end.

Joq shrugged, tried to play it cool. "Of course." What he really wanted to say, what he really couldn't believe, was that George wasn't addressing the Finn sized elephant in the room.

"Cool," George breathed out. "It's just. I can't... talk like you do."

Ah, yes you fucking well can, Joq bit his tongue on that retort.

"It's really fine."

"Cool," George said again and looked back at his hands.

"So, we're cool?" Joq heard his desperation, but he couldn't take it back.

"Course, why wouldn't we be? I mean, if you're cool that I'm, you know, doing that now too, then of course," George stood.

"Uh, yeah, but I mean..."

What did he mean? He meant: I fuck different guys. Hundreds of them. Joq was pretty damn sure George was planning to continue to fuck one other guy. One other guy George clearly had feelings for. Joq didn't know how to come out and say that.

"You mean?" George asked. He was standing, his expression guarded.

"Just, you know, be careful or whatever."

"What's that supposed to mean?"

"Nothing," Joq shook his head.

"I'm using protection," George said.

Joq almost let the 'yeah, I saw that,' slip, but held it in.

"Good, I knew you would. Good."

George shook his head, "Okay, well, I just wanted to tell you 'cos that's what the agreement was. So, yeah," and then he was walking out.

"I'm just saying," Joq said before George had left the room. "If it's Finn, be careful."

George's step faltered. He didn't look at Joq, and Joq wasn't looking at him.

"I know what the deal is," George said so softly, Joq had to look at him.

George was looking at the hallway, a pained expression on his face. Then he buried it, shot Joq a tight smile and walked out.

24

J OQ FELT SOMETHING SHIFT in their home life after that. It was
  easier, with the truth, or part of it, out there, and harder, with the
reality of that truth in his face.

"Heading out?" he asked George later that week when he saw him
in front of the mirror, his hand running through his hair to style it, his
good cologne mixing with the smell of his skin in that enticing way it
did after a shower.

"Yeah," George met his eyes in the mirror and gave him a self-deprecating smile. "Gonna grab a bite."

Joq nodded, smiled. Before, he'd assume it was team stuff. He tried
to remember if George used to tell him or if Joq had always assumed.

George kissed him on the side of the head, his "Don't wait up," also
a familiar line, wrong in the new context.

All Joq could think when he heard George drive up the following
morning at dawn was, well, at least he took his advice. He rolled over
and went back to sleep.

It was midway through the season, on the cusp of the business end, when Joq felt so agitated by this new normal he decided to do something about it. He and George hadn't had sex in the month since George started up with Finn. Joq got laid nonetheless—and George clearly got laid judging by the contented glow he radiated when he came home from his little outings; he must've been fucking Finn like a dog in heat. But sex was the glue that kept them together. They needed to make more of an effort.

This backfired spectacularly when George failed to stay hard.

"Have you been drinking?" Joq asked after popping his mouth off George's softening dick. He knew George was sober.

George rubbed his eyes. He was leaning against the headboard, naked and stretched out, the powerful physique that usually turned Joq's cranks now turning him off. He shoved that idea away and focused on working his hand up and down George's length, his saliva slicking the way.

"No," George groaned and rocked into his hand.

He had a semi at least. Joq leaned down to take him in his mouth again. George slid his hand into Joq's hair and tried to grip it as he rocked his hips up. Joq's hair was short, so George's rough fingers gripped clumsily at his head instead.

"Ah, fuck," George said and pulled his hips back so he was slipping out of Joq's mouth. "I can't turn my head off."

Joq sat up, wiped his mouth with the back of his hand.

George grabbed the blankets and covered himself. He ran a hand through his hair.

"Sorry," he said, his eyes flicking to Joq's then away.

There was a lot Joq wanted to say, but some alarm bell in him said to tread carefully.

He shrugged. "We haven't fucked in a month. Don't reckon that's ever happened," he cracked a smile.

George snorted. "It hasn't."

Joq got up and grabbed his pyjama pants, tugged them on and got back in his side of the bed. George shuffled over, breathing loudly beside him.

"It's the season, it's, you know. A lot."

Joq shook his head. "It's not the season," he said quietly.

George rubbed his face. "It's just... new. You know?"

Joq felt the atmosphere in the room charge. They were talking about it. The moment felt fragile, important.

"I get it," he said carefully.

"It's just fucking, but," George glanced at him like he was checking if it was alright to go on. Joq tipped his head in acknowledgement.

"It's..."

"It's?" Joq asked, unable to curb his impatience.

George huffed. "You know," he waved a hand, breaking the moment with the movement. "I mean, *you* know. You do this all the time."

"Yeah," Joq replied. "It'll wear off."

George frowned. He looked away.

"Yeah, he'll get sick of it soon enough. And I'll, you know... as well," George got up, snagged his pants off the floor. "Nothing to worry about," he dragged a hand through his hair and went for the door.

"Where're you going?"

"Water," George called over his shoulder.

He had a glass of water on his bedside table.

Joq was so distracted by it when he went into work later that week, he almost walked straight into Alison when he entered the break room.

"Sorry," he said and just managed to not spill his coffee all over her.

"No, sorry, that was all me. Lurking, sorry," she smiled up at him.

He smiled back and went to step around her.

"I've got something," she said as Joq went to the sink to grab a cloth for the spillage on the mug. "I think you should have it."

"Hmmm," Joq wiped the mug, took a big sip.

"I erased it from the hard drive, but I downloaded a copy first. For you," she went on. She was nervous.

Joq turned. It was then he realised the time, and thought to wonder what she was doing here hours before she needed to be. Hours before anyone else would be. At the hour when Joq always came in.

She was watching him steadily, her appearance the professional, tidy one she always had—mousy hair in a pony tail, eyes calm, black pants and white button-up tucked in, her suit jacket loose on her diminutive frame—but there was a defiance in her this morning too, and a hint of nerves.

"What's for me?" he asked.

She came forward and held up a thumb drive. "I was on call for security last night and... Here," she handed it over.

Joq took it, looked at the red plastic in his palm.

"You should watch that, then..."

He looked up, she was watching him steadily, and he recognised the defiance for what it was in a moment of clarity—loyalty.

He closed his palm.

"Thank you."

She breathed out. "You're welcome. I'm gonna go get coffee, maybe something to eat."

"Okay."

"I'll be back for my shift."

"Okay."

She nodded like something had been settled, grabbed her handbag and left.

Joq opened his palm and looked at the USB.

He went into the security room, gave the monitors a cursory glance; the emptiness of the building spread before him like his own personal empire. Sliding his laptop out of his bag, he opened it, typed in his password and held the thumb drive at the portal. He looked at the screensaver, the blinding grins he and George wore, sat back, and tapped the USB on the desk.

Joq was still tapping the desk, his screen black, when he heard the beep of the alarm deactivate on the other side of the door, the sucking sound as it opened.

"Hey, boss," Simo grinned at him as he came in, hands full of his breakfast of a Macca's bag and a shake.

"You're in early," Joq replied and slid his palm around the USB.

Simo gave him a funny look. "It's nine."

"Oh," Joq shut his laptop, put it in his bag and slid the USB into the front pocket. "Must've zoned out."

Simo chuckled as he took his seat, sipped on his straw. "Ain't surprised, not much doin' here. You want me to check the messages?"

"Yeah," Joq breathed out and followed Simo's gaze to the blinking red light that meant a call had been registered with the external security company overnight.

Simo hit play. Joq ran a hand through his hair and decided he wasn't going to look at that footage. The tinny sound of the security officer came through the speaker informing them an alarm had been tripped overnight but they'd spoken to Mr Creed on-site, nothing to worry about.

"Weird," Simo said and bit into his muffin.

The door beeped again and Alison pushed in. Joq met her concerned expression. He shook his head minutely and she nodded like she got it.

"Mornin', Ali," Simo said around a mouthful.

"How many times, Simo?" she replied as she took a seat.

Simo laughed and spun to face the screens. "Alison, Miss Alison. Good morning."

"Morning," she cracked a smile and took her seat.

"Alright," Joq sat up. "Let's get that camera outside the trainer's room fixed today, Simo?"

"On it."

"And Alison, can you run Sue through the game day drill when she gets in at noon? We want to tighten that up before finals."

"Of course."

"You don't wanna check last night?" Simo asked. "Security left a message," he said to Alison.

"I'll do it later," Joq said and stood. "I've got a meeting with the front office. Let me know how you go with the camera," he finished and went out, his bag firmly on his shoulder, his hand tight on the strap.

Physically, he was in that meeting and he finished up the day, pretty sure everything was running well. The team was good. Sue, Alison and Simo worked well together; each took responsibility for their role and he felt like he could trust them.

As he hit the button for the gate, saw the bumper of George's car, he thought for the first time he couldn't say if he felt the same for George. He suppressed that thought quickly—George had been honest with him.

The problem was Joq was starting to feel like a fool. And that was making an unfamiliar form of anger simmer just below the surface.

He clicked the door shut and George called out, "In the kitchen," and Joq felt himself close down.

"Hey," he said as he walked in.

"Hey, babe," George replied as he shot him a warm smile and then went back to whatever he was making. It was not stir-fry and a cookbook was open.

"What's all this?" Joq asked. He cocked his hip against the bench, folded his arms over his chest.

"Thought I'd try and cook you something different," George winked.

Joq felt part of his anger abate, and a crack of guilt come in.

"Yeah?"

"Yeah," George smiled, closed mouthed but warm, and went back to some kind of fillet he had marinating in a bowl, before he took it out and rolled it in crumbs. "It might suck balls, but I can always correct next time."

Joq snorted. "Okay, coach," he went for the fridge.

"I got the wine you like," George said and Joq saw a bottle of his favourite Sauvignon blanc and a six-pack of the ciders he'd been ordering when they went out next to it.

Joq grabbed a cider, cracked it, and went over to the window to look at the pool. He listened to George behind him, hummed when George started talking about the team's chances now they were almost certain to make the final eight, and tried his best to shake the remnants of his anger, tried to break out of the shell of indifference he felt himself encased in.

"Looks good," Joq said when they sat down at the long dining table inside.

George gave him a grateful smile. They ate. It almost felt normal. The food was good, surprisingly so, and Joq couldn't help the genuine way he felt when he told George, "You been holding out on me."

George laughed it off, cleared the table, and finished his water.

By the time they went to bed, Joq had almost forgotten about the existence of Finn. He was beginning to wonder if he'd imagined the invisible strain between him and George.

George wrapped his arms around him, pressed his hardening dick against Joq's ass.

"Not tonight," Joq heard himself say and didn't understand why, but he knew he was definitely not in the mood.

"Really?" George asked, surprised. But he was quick to let Joq go and roll onto his back, his hand still on Joq's hip, squeezing reassuringly.

"Yeah, long day, management, you know? They want bag checks on game days, security scanners..." Joq heard himself rambling.

"Hmmm," George sounded sleepy when Joq finally petered out.

"George?" Joq asked a while later.

George didn't reply, his hand lax on Joq's hip, his breathing deep and even. Joq couldn't sleep, his mind turning over the evening, that USB in his bag taunting him, the remnants of that quiet anger still simmering as he berated himself to let it go.

25

G EORGE WAS DOING LAPS when Joq got up the next morning. The coffee was already made, the house toasty warm with the heaters on, and the soft glow of the lamps made the place feel cosy against the dark chill of the early morning outside.

As Joq watched, he thought George must've changed the pool to warm; he always did it around this time, switched between going for a run and doing laps. He drank his coffee, thought about all this and couldn't fathom a world where they broke up. His original thinking had been right: let it play out. Don't look at that USB stick. In fact, he should destroy it. It was none of his business.

"Cold?" he asked when George came in.

"Nah," George grinned. "Heater works a treat."

"Training?"

"Yeah," George looked at the clock, rubbed his head with the towel. "I better hustle, you workin' tonight?"

"Yeah," Joq turned to refill his mug. "Afternoon shift then I've got this bloody meeting with the security scanner group near the airport."

"Why can't they come to us?"

Joq shrugged. "Guess it's easier. But hey, you can cook now, so."

George smiled and flicked Joq with his towel as he went past. "I'll wait up."

"Okay," Joq returned the smile and felt the relief. So, George wasn't planning to hook up with Finn tonight. That was good, maybe it was already playing itself out. It'd been over a month, George had probably had his fill, realised what he had with Joq was deeper, more, real.

Joq felt that was confirmed when he watched them on the security monitor after training that afternoon. George went over to Finn in the locker room, hands gesticulating as he explained something. Finn's face was serious, concentrating, before he turned back to getting changed and George wandered off to talk to another player.

It was about as normal and boring as it got between a player and a coach.

Joq exhaled. He told Sue he was heading to this meeting, he wouldn't be back, and could she finish up. She assured him she could, again with the tone that said a monkey could do it, and he didn't bother hiding his smile.

He was halfway to their offices when he got a call to reschedule.

"Fuck's sake," he said after he ended the call. He needed to get off the highway, turn around, and battle peak hour traffic going the other way.

By the time he pulled up behind George's car, he felt the excessive relief that can only come from having to sit in traffic and drive for over an hour to get back, the sight of that car telling him he was truly home.

As he shut the front door, hung up his keys, shrugged off his coat, and kicked off his shoes, he could tell George wasn't in the house. Joq smiled when he realised he was in the pool again. George always got inordinately excited for the first few days when he switched it to heated.

Joq was about to call out around his smile, his socked feet quiet on the tiles as he came up to the open sliding doors and saw the pool still in front of him. He froze when he saw them, the scene so explicit it was like his brain couldn't comprehend what it was seeing.

They were in the cabana, bodies wound tightly together as they fucked. The night was still, quiet, and the sound of George's hips slapping into Finn's groin, George's groans, Finn's panting breaths as he spread his legs wider to take George's dick deeper seemed louder than it probably was.

Joq stepped back on some instinct. Then froze. There was no way they could see him from where he was in the shadows just beyond the door. Not that they would look, he thought as he watched the way George's thumbs stroked Finn's cheekbones, kissed him gently in counterpoint to the way he was thrusting so deeply into him. George's eyes were open as he gazed at Finn, and Finn watched him back, his breaths stuttering as he took everything George was giving him.

Something twisted inside Joq's gut. He couldn't look away. He couldn't move.

Finn's board shorts were hanging off one leg, like they'd gotten started in a rush and couldn't even be bothered to undress properly; George's own shorts were tucked under his ass like he'd just managed to get his dick out. Their bodies were wet, their hair drenched, like they'd moved from the pool to the cabana to fuck on a flat surface.

Joq was affronted not just by the sight, but by the fact they were fucking outside. The walls were high and the place was private; but

George always resisted when Joq worked him up out there—"Long lenses," he'd say, as if some photographer would bother stalking out a football player in his home.

Now though? Now George was fucking his rookie in the open like he couldn't have stopped himself if the entire media room at a post-game press conference was there.

"Good?" George asked softly.

Joq could hear it clearly in the stillness of the night.

"So good," Finn panted.

"Yeah? Love that dick, baby?" George said around a sexy smile as he rammed in harder, kissed Finn's throat.

"Just yours," Finn gasped. "Just, fuck. Yours."

Joq sucked in a breath and stepped back like he'd been slapped. That little fucking shit.

"Yeah," George said, his voice turning serious. "Just mine." And then he started grinding in deeper, fucking Finn so hard the litany of Finn's, "Yours, just yours," punched out of him between sharp breaths.

Joq felt his whole body light up with a mix of enraged jealousy and blinding desire. He was watching the most intimate sex he'd ever seen—sue him, he was getting fucking hard.

"Fuck, please," Finn gasped and threw his head back. George kissed his collar bones, squeezed a hand between their bodies and started to jerk him off.

"Gonna come on my dick, baby?" George said against Finn's lips.

Finn brought his hands down, gripped George's ass and tugged him in. He looked right into George's eyes as he rocked underneath him, "Just yours."

Jesus. Joq spun around and went down the hall, the sound of their fucking loud behind him. He almost crashed into the side table as he went for the door to get into the gym bathroom.

He stumbled in the dark into the room, got his hand on his dick, and jerked off franticly to the sight behind his eyelids. He felt the strangest orgasm building fast—he was coiled with a lust out of his control, but the feeling was saturated in jealousy. He came in his hand and bit back the sound. Not that he needed to worry they'd hear him.

He stood there and caught his breath. He needed to go back out. He needed to act normal. He needed to confront them. What he really wanted to do was leave. He knew he wouldn't.

He washed his hands, flicked on the light and looked at himself in the mirror. He was flushed, but otherwise normal enough. He waited.

Then, he went back out. He could hear them in the pool, the water lapping gently at the side. He was about to force out the cheerful, surprised, "Hey," when he stopped again.

They were in the pool, wrapped up in each other, kissing.

"Hi," burst out of him, too loud.

He watched as they sprung back.

"Joq, hey," George recovered first. "That was quick."

"Cancelled," he forced out, shoved his hands in his pockets and smiled what he hoped was a smile that said he hadn't seen them fucking like porn stars in love, nor had he jerked off about it in the bathroom.

He glanced at Finn. Finn was bright red, his smile sheepish, his wide eyes nervous.

"Hi, Joq," he said though, relaxed.

Joq had a sudden desire to punch him in his stupidly gorgeous face.

"Hi," he said instead. "Mind if I join you?" he heard himself asking.

Finn did not school the frown that flashed across his face. But George was answering.

"Course. Nice and warm," he said, exceedingly cheerful.

"Cool, I'll go change."

They were a careful distance apart when Joq came back out, both looking his way with forced smiles when he stepped through the glass doors. Joq took the steps nearest George, felt his own smile straining as he said, "Warm."

"Can't believe you've got a heated pool," Finn said and Joq glanced up at his smiling face, his eyes on George, his voice forcing a semblance of normal into the conversation.

"I like to swim all year round," George said.

"Yeah, same," Finn leaned back, his head resting on the edge, eyes on the sky.

Joq felt like he was intruding. He moved over to George and leaned in to kiss him. George caught on a moment too late and the kiss was as awkward as everything else about this.

He heard the rush of water at the same time as Finn was saying, "I better go."

"No, don't go, I've defrosted steaks—

Joq cut George off. "You got a problem with a bit of PDA between boyfriends?"

"Joq," George said like he was reprimanding an errant player.

"What?" Joq held his hands up.

"Course not," Finn mumbled.

He was out of the pool now, reaching for his shorts, his naked body on display in all its perfect glory.

The moment felt unbearably uncomfortable, but within that, Joq felt fucking angry. Finn was a fuck, nothing more. They all needed to remember that.

"Why the rush then? Stay for dinner," Joq said.

"I've got, I forgot," Finn hiked his shorts up his thighs, over his ass, his eyes on his hands fastening the laces, "plans," he finished lamely and reached for his hoodie.

"I'll walk you out," George said and was getting out of the pool before Joq could say anything.

He watched as George grabbed his own shorts and pulled them on quickly, Finn waiting next to him and looking anywhere but at Joq, at George, at the pool.

"Later, Finn," Joq said.

Finn smiled at his feet, waved, and didn't look back as he went ahead and George followed.

Joq sighed and swam for a bit. He dropped under the water. When he resurfaced, he expected George to be there. He wasn't. Joq got out, wrapped a towel around himself and went into the kitchen. He could hear them in the hallway, their voices quiet. Joq crept closer.

"You know we're together. And someday you'll find someone—

"Stop saying that!" Finn cut George off. He was keeping his voice down, but he was definitely angry.

"It's true," George said, hushed but firm. "You're still so young, you don't get it."

"You were eighteen when you got together with *him*," Finn hissed.

"It's different," George said. "We were both young. Someday you'll meet someone your own age and you'll..." Joq could hear how he couldn't even finish the sentence.

"Yeah, okay," Finn sounded really mad now. The door opened. "Go fuck your boyfriend then."

The door slammed and something crashed into it. Joq's eyes widened when he realised what he was hearing—George had stopped Finn from leaving and was now clearly kissing him up against the door. He could hear Finn moaning into the kiss, the sound of George shoving him into the wood, then the sound of their combined panting breaths as they broke apart.

"I just..." George whispered.

"You just what?" Finn sounded desperate.

Joq found himself desperately hanging on to hear what George had to say as well. George didn't say anything, just breathed heavily.

"You should go," George said after a long moment.

Joq could hear nothing but their breathing and then the sound of the door opening and closing. He backed up into the kitchen and opened the fridge.

George came in and met Joq's eyes. He sighed.

"How much did you hear?" he asked.

Joq slammed the fridge. "Enough."

George shook his head, folded his arms over his chest.

"Are you in love with him?" Joq was proud of himself for getting the question out there.

"I..." George looked lost for a second. He shut it down. "No," he said firmly. "It's a crush. It's just fucking. It's the season, it's intense," he waved his hand.

Joq nodded his head, but all he could hear was that suspended moment of "I...", and all he could see was the lost look on George's face.

"I'm gonna shower," Joq said and went to go past him.

George stopped him with a hand on his bicep. "It's just fucking."

Joq wondered who he was trying to convince.

He jerked his chin and shrugged out of the hold. "You might want to tell him that," he said and left George in the kitchen.

George's soft, "Yeah," was a moment too late and barely audible.

26

J OQ HAD A NEW habit. He'd take the USB stick out of his bag, roll
it in his hand, and put it back. He knew he needed to watch it. He
couldn't bring himself to watch it. He was in the middle of this little
routine in his office at home when he heard George come in.

"Joq?" he called up the stairs.

"In here," Joq shoved the USB stick into the pocket and spun in his
chair.

"Hey," George smiled when he came in. "What're you doing?"

Joq shrugged. He supposed it did look weird, him sitting there with
his laptop closed, the room dark and quiet.

"Well, ah," George ran a hand through his hair and looked around.
He'd been doing a version of this since the night with Finn and the
pool—acting sheepish, being around more, accommodating when he
was.

It'd only been a week and it felt like a lifetime of awkward.

"Did you want something?" Joq asked when George didn't go on.

"Just wanted to see if you wanted to go see a movie. I've got that
away game, then Freo the week after and they've got Reaver back, so
I'm gonna be all systems go thinking how to shut him down—

"Jack's back?" Joq cut him off.

Jack Reaver had been the upcoming superstar rookie when George was in his glory veteran days. Team mates and good friends, George never quite forgave Jack for requesting the trade back to his home city. Joq, on the other hand, had very fond memories of Jack for a very different reason. Jack was, like George, one hundred percent gay, one hundred percent in the closet. He and Joq had never done anything—Joq drew the line at his age, and him being a fellow player with George—but God, the flirting had been fun. He genuinely liked him too, as a person, and as a player.

"Yeah," George said, grimacing. "Looks like the season-ending injury wasn't so season-ending."

"Huh, good for him."

"You know, I'm really beginning to wonder whose side you're on this season," he smiled as he said it.

Joq shrugged again. He was wondering the same thing. "What? He's a good guy, so he wanted to go home. It wasn't personal."

George mumbled about how he could've waited another season or two and besides, what'd he done since going home other than get spectacularly injured?

"And play some spectacular games with Hiller before that," Joq said.

George snorted.

"What?"

"Nothin', movies yes or no? I feel like some mindless action."

"Uh, yeah, okay. But what's the deal with Hiller?"

George tapped his knuckles on the doorframe. "I mean, yeah, they team up well, but watch closer next time. I know you know Jack," and that was pointed, which was pretty fucking rich. But George went on over Joq's scoffing. "Hiller's got a hate-on for him so hard,"

George shook his head and backed out, "sometimes I think it's taking everything Jack's got not to cry about it. Movie starts at eight-twenty."

And then he was gone. Huh, Joq thought, at least that was a nice little distraction. He'd be sure to watch and see how Jack acted around Sean Hiller, see if there was anything in it.

In the meantime, he needed to go to the movies with his boyfriend, where he'd pretend George wasn't his boyfriend. Among other things he was currently pretending about. He pulled the USB stick out again and rolled it in his palm.

27

♥

JOQ LAY IN BED that night and listened to George sleeping beside him. His breaths seemed louder than usual and it prevented Joq from drifting off. He wondered if George had always breathed so loudly.

The movie had been unsatisfying. All the right cues were there, but it felt disjointed, like it'd been slapped together out of the requirements—reluctant hero forced to save the world—without any further thought. A shallow spin on the original. Much like he felt with George sitting beside him in the cinema. The careful space between them, the buddies routine they'd been doing for over a decade—for the first time, it felt less like an exciting secret Joq got to break when he got home, and more like a stupid pretence designed to protect George's precious sense of his own self-importance.

Joq slipped out of bed. He was never going to sleep with these thoughts ticking over, with George's obnoxious breathing. He went out to the hall and paused. He thought about that USB and felt a surge of anger at how much it was consuming him. He shook himself and went to the kitchen, grabbed a beer, went into the living room and sprawled on the couch.

He clicked on the TV and snorted a humourless laugh when he saw it was a late night replay of the Talking Heads footy show with none other than Finn as the guest. What were the fucking chances? He took a swig and sat back, remote clutched in one hand, beer in the other.

Finn was leaning back on one of the couches, two of the hosts on the couch opposite, and another older one beside him. The old guy was a legend of the game, brought on to class this trash up and give a decent opinion. The other two, while knowledgeable, generally asked mundane personal questions and injected the odd remark on the style of play of whatever player was a guest that night.

The screen behind the couch had one of the photos of Finn and his sister from his social media. She was in a string bikini, Finn in loose boardshorts and nothing else, their matching grins with blinding white teeth against tan skin and dancing blue eyes met the camera.

"*Yeah, that's Soph,*" Finn was saying, craning his head back to look at the picture. His smile was easy, not a hint of embarrassment at the producers selection of a rather revealing picture. Finn looked at it, then back at the guys like it was a normal family photo.

"*She's older?*" the younger of the hosts asked. He was the TV man, not so much a football man.

Finn smirked. "*By a few seconds.*"

"*Oh,*" the guy laughed and looked back at the picture. "*Why did we think she was older?*"

"*Think she edited my Wikipedia page,*" Finn replied and gave the guy a knowing smile when he looked back at Finn and laughed again, caught. Finn smiled at him like it was okay and explained that yes, they were twins, yes she came out first, and yes, she liked having that over him.

"*So, you're not worried about her being around all these other players?*"

Finn cracked another sly grin. "*I reckon I'd be more worried for any guy Soph was with than the other way round.*"

The hosts laughed and Finn leaned back. They went on in an imitation of banter, and Joq again hated to admit how likeable Finn was; how even under the loose script, he seemed genuine—his lazy smile and sleepy eyes twinkled like he knew something you didn't. For all his youth, he could pull off the solidity of a man in a way that was unsettling.

The show moved on to one of those stupid activities they had players do—try and handball a football through a hole on a large, spinning wheel—and Finn participated good-naturedly, consoling the TV man as he messed it up, calling his own success, "*Beginner's luck*," and generally doing a good job of the PR exercise.

He was certainly not fully himself; he had the guarded persona all players put on when they went on these shows, friendly yet professional and private, but he was easy in it, and he seemed to sincerely want to put the presenters at ease and make a good show for them. His young eyes widened with ironic joy as they gave him a plastic trophy for making three successful shots, and he reverently placed the toy on the coffee table when they sat back down.

Joq took a swig of his beer. Finn was running a hand through his blonde hair as he sat back, smiling politely over at the older guy beside him as he started to speak.

"*There's been a lot of talk about Creed's ascension to Head Coach.*"

Finn nodded, his expression turning serious.

"*Now, I know Creed,*" the old guy went on. "*Hell of a player, hell of a player,*" he shook his head like he was in the memory, "*but coaching ain't playing and while he's got you boys as finals contenders, I gotta wonder if you'd a done it without him anyway. You got the side for it.*"

Finn was already shaking his head. "*It's all George.*"

"*Come on now,*" the old guy sat forward, started counting on his fingers, "*you got Lacy down there makin' those same plays he's been doin since he was playin' with George last season—*

"*Sorry,*" Finn cut him off, his quick smile apologetic, "*but look closer. George put Lacy down there. He's moved me and the rest of the mid-field to work with Lacy without taxing Lacy all over the ground.*"

"*Yeah, but, you get a player like Lacy, like yourself, you're gonna do that anyway.*"

Finn was shaking his head. "*You don't get it.*"

The other two presenters made scoffing noises and Joq had to agree—it was a bit rich, a rookie trying to school a legend, but Finn just smiled at them all, his expression serious over that. "*George sees every player. He like, sees us. And he's not afraid to go old school if he sees that'd work better for that player.*"

Joq thought about watching them in that hotel room. About what Finn had said about the game, and he felt like a whole series of conversations had taken place in that vein. He could almost see it—the mutual love of the game, the shared vision and understanding, the way George would've been able to take what Finn said and build it into a strategy for the team.

"*Okay, okay,*" the old guy was nodding, "*I can see that, I can see that.*"

"*He's still a bit green to be Head Coach though,*" the TV guy said.

Finn shot him a smile; nothing friendly in it. "*And when we make final four? Is he still gonna be too green then?*"

"*With you on the side, Finnegan,*" the regular presenter interjected, "*you were always gonna make final four.*"

"*And that's where George gets what you don't,*" Finn replied. For the first time, he didn't seem like the young, boyish rookie hamming it up for a PR exercise—he seemed like a young man who knew his shit, who respected his coach, trusted him, and was willing to go to war over it.

It was disorientating for a late night footy show meant as a humorous diversion. And it was a side to Finn Joq was pretty sure no one in the footy world had seen. He found himself sitting forward, watching Finn on screen staring the guy down.

"*Oh yeah?*" the TV man said, smirking. Joq got the feeling he was trying to act like he was lightening the mood but what he really wanted to do was make Finn look like a stupid boy.

"*It's about the team. We're a team,*" Finn said completely unruffled, undeterred. "*George sees each of us as individuals and then puts us together like a single organism that works. Sure, I'm a valuable piece, but you're playing to lose if you build an entire team around one player. George doesn't do that favourites stuff like you do. He knows all of us, and he values all of us. We all feel it, and we all respect him because of it. It's not fake, it's real. He's a bloody brilliant coach, and I'm honoured to play for him.*"

Joq's eyebrows went up. That was a bit much for a player to say on a coach. The presenters looked flabbergasted as well, but the old guy was nodding along.

"*Finnegan makes a good point,*" he began, like this was a normal way to talk, "*it reminds me of Hawthorn in the eighties, and we really saw the truth of a great team versus a great player in that Grand Final against Geelong ...*"

Joq stopped listening. He was looking at Finn, who was nodding along to the old guy, but he was flushed, worked up. Players supported their coaches, nothing unusual in that if the team worked well. But Joq thought Finn's little speech was bordering on uncomfortable; it came off like naïve devotion to a leader or something else.

It was the something else that really bothered Joq.

Joq barely slept, and he was sitting in the kitchen with a coffee the next morning when George came in before dawn.

"Oh, hey," George said when he saw him. "You're up early."

George grabbed a smoothie from the fridge, a water, continued in his motions for starting the day while shooting Joq a smile.

"Couldn't sleep."

"Hmmm," George said. "Thought you were gonna fall asleep in the cinema," he smiled as he zipped up his training bag.

Joq huffed a laugh because he felt like he should.

"I caught the footy show, with Finn."

George shouldered his bag and looked at Joq, frowned. "Did you come to bed at all?"

Joq ignored that. "Have you seen it?"

"Uh, yeah," George replied and ran a hand through his hair. "Thought he did well. Those things always suck, you know that."

"You didn't think he was a bit, you know..."

George raised an eyebrow. "A bit what?"

Joq shook his head. "You know, George, come on," he got up and refilled his coffee.

"I reckon you're gonna have to tell me," George replied.

Joq glanced at him. George was giving him a blank look. Joq couldn't tell if it was deliberate obtuseness, or he genuinely didn't see Finn declaring his devotion on TV as a problem.

Joq turned and leaned against the bench, sipped his coffee. "It was a bit much, he might want to tone it down."

George looked at him with surprise. "After all the shit I've had thrown at me this season, I reckon having my star player come out in support is a good thing. I'd have thought you'd agree."

Joq gave him an incredulous look. "I might if you weren't fucking him."

George's lips parted. "What's that got to do with it?"

"Really?"

"Yeah, really," George hoisted his bag up his shoulder. "We can separate this stuff."

"Really," Joq heard the sarcasm and prepared for an argument.

But George just shook his head, smiled like he got something Joq didn't. "Yeah, really. Look, I gotta go, I'll call you when we get there."

He came over and kissed Joq on the temple. "You're reading too much into shit," he said quietly.

Joq sighed. "Yeah, maybe."

"Yeah, definitely. Finn's got a good eye for the game and even if we weren't, you know," George said as he moved away, "I'd be interested in what he thinks."

"He should still tone it down," Joq muttered.

George stopped in the doorway. "Christ, why?"

"'Cos you don't want to be out!"

George recoiled. Like it'd never crossed his mind having his rookie moonshining all over him on national TV, while also taking his dick like a pro on a regular basis, could lead to that. And maybe it couldn't, and maybe Joq was paranoid. But the something that bothered him was that Finn could go on national TV, have George's back so thoroughly, and no one batted an eye.

"I really don't think that's gonna happen," George said after a minute with quiet conviction. "I gotta... Don't worry about that, alright?"

"I'm just trying to protect you," Joq said and felt like he was lying.

"I know," George nodded like he believed him. "I'll talk to you later."

And then he was gone.

Joq got ready for work, then sat at his desk. He didn't have to be in for hours and it wasn't busy with the team travelling. He could practically feel the USB stick taunting him, as if the little piece of plastic was imbued with every paranoid thought and possibility. It pissed him off no end and he really wanted to stop thinking about it—

His phone rang. George.

"Hello?"

"Hey," George said, his voice clipped but not angry; he was in a hurry. "Just wanted to call before we left."

"Oh, okay," Joq leaned back in his chair, took a deep breath. "You good?"

"Yeah, all good. Just... thought that was kinda shitty this morning."

"What was?"

"That conversation."

"Yeah," Joq breathed out. "Well, maybe I'm reading too much into it—

"You are."

"But," Joq went on forcefully, "I meant what I said, I'm just trying to protect you."

Joq heard himself, knew it was a lie, and wondered why he was doubling down on it.

"And I appreciate it, but, and I can't believe I'm the one saying it this time..."

Joq could practically see the smile in George's voice—the small one, the old couple one that said it's you and me and we're in this together.

"But you're being paranoid."

Joq drummed his fingers on the desk. Actually, he was being ridiculous. Paranoid was putting it nicely. But he was beginning to feel like he was losing control, like he was slipping into saying things he wouldn't have dreamed he'd say.

"Joq?"

"Yeah, yeah, I'm here, sorry."

"Just, go have some fun while I'm away, okay?"

Joq snorted. He really didn't feel like doing that.

"You too I guess," he muttered.

George sighed. "I gotta go. We're good, yeah?"

"Yeah, call me from the hotel."

"I will. Later."

"Bye."

The line went dead.

Joq had a feeling if he kept pushing this, it was going to end very badly. He pulled the USB stick out of his bag, looked at it, and tossed it in the bin.

28

SITTING IN THE SURVEILLANCE room later that morning, Joq half-heartedly watched the screens and listened to Sue explaining to Simo that if he kept eating like he was, he was going to have a coronary—"Just because you're skinny, doesn't mean it's not killing you on the inside."

Joq snorted, but his heart wasn't in it.

Simo guffawed and gave his usual line: "Every man dies, but not every man truly lives!"

Joq's phone buzzed.

A message from his mum. He opened it.

It's doing the rounds again... He should make a statement this time.

Joq clicked on the attachment. He knew what it would be and it was. That old rumour nicely packaged in an article with the usual suspects from around the world. Another gay blog, though this one was inching closer to mainstream. His mum had a point—well, beyond her usual point about George not being man enough to stand beside her boy—but her other point being, every other athlete on here had responded in some way over the years except George.

Joq forwarded it and, in light of their conversation that morning, felt oddly triumphant as he waited for George to reply.

Seen it, came back immediately.

Joq frowned. The triumph wavered as a quiet sense of foreboding came over him.

But, he was a dutiful boyfriend: *You okay?*

All good.

Joq didn't know what to say to that. Over the years, George ignored the rumour stoically, but he'd borne an undercurrent of terror whenever it came up. Joq wanted to be there for him and yet, he'd felt responsible somehow. Guilty. Which was stupid, but it made it impossible for him to discuss it, to help.

If you wanna talk...

He sent anyway, cringed, and waited.

It'll blow over, came back promptly and when the next message came through—*Boarding*—Joq felt like the door blew firmly shut with it.

29

G EORGE WAS LAUGHING, TINNY through the speakers, his face
filling the screen on his laptop from where he was perched on
his bed in a hotel room in Sydney.

"You shoulda seen it though, babe," George went on and Joq felt
butterflies at the endearment; it'd dropped off lately, and it was nice,
reassuring. "Lacy was livid!"

One of the vets had got him good with the old—'Hey, can I borrow your toilet, someone's using mine?' and then taken a huge shit,
stinking out his entire room.

"He's been around long enough not to fall for that," Joq said and
leaned back in his office chair at home.

"I know, I know," George petered out. He was smiling and talking
like the article hadn't come out that morning, like he'd genuinely
squared it away and firmly closed the door on discussing it. "What're
you up to tonight? You look tired."

Joq didn't get to answer because there was a knock on George's
door.

George frowned. "Hang on."

He was up and out of view, but Joq could hear Finn's voice clear
enough. "Hey, you busy?"

"Just talking to Joq," George said, his voice coming closer, the door clicking shut. "Thought you were going out with the SANFL guys?"

"I was," Finn leaned down and waved at the screen; that stupid little wave he always did. "Am. Hey, Joq."

"Finn," Joq smiled. It felt like he smiled.

"Just, Danny texted about going to some club," Joq couldn't see much beyond their groins, but he could see Finn plucking at his button-up. "I think this is too dressy? Can I borrow one of yours?"

"Sure," George said, then leaned back to the screen. "I'll call you tomorrow. Make sure you go for us."

Joq laughed, uneasy. "I'll think about it."

"You do that," George smiled and then he must've slammed the laptop shut.

Joq sat back. Did Finn really need a shirt? Was that transparent as fuck or was Joq completely paranoid?

Were they fucking in that hotel room right now? Worse, kissing before Finn went out for the night with the promise to return to George's bed later? Worse still, were they cuddling and kissing on the bed while they watched some replay together? Even worse: was George confiding in fucking Finn about that article?

Fuck it. Joq pulled the USB stick out of the bin, plugged it into the portal and opened it. There was one video file. He clicked on it. His hand had a faint tremor.

"Jesus," he said out loud. *You know they're fucking, you know they're fucking like that, nothing new is gonna be seen here.*

He took a deep breath and watched. The screen was dark, but Joq made out the oval at the centre of the stadium. Empty. No, someone was in the middle. The lights came on: a blinding explosion of light.

Finn was in the middle of the oval, football in hand, his smile growing as he looked somewhere off to the side. George appeared, jogging over to him, his brown hair wavy and bouncing, his answering smile moving around whatever he was saying as he came closer. Finn bounced the ball, said something, then took off, heading for the goals, George charging hard behind him.

Joq had forgotten how magnificent George looked when he played. He settled in to watch and all they did was play. Kicking to each other, kicking on goal, and okay, George lifted Finn with a bit too much enthusiasm when he kicked a belter from the fifty metre mark, and Finn's hands were on George's ass a little too much when he tackled him, but unless someone was actually looking for it, there was nothing in it.

He watched as they both looked up at the same time. The security guard. George jogged over. Then he was signing an autograph for the guy, Finn ambling over to do the same.

There was nothing in it. Nothing other than an inappropriate training session one on one between a coach and his star rookie. But even that was arguable.

The video jump cut to them heading down the tunnel, friendly hip and shoulders, mouths moving as they talked.

Joq realised Alison had edited this. She'd been on call. She'd taken the security call. She knew it was George. She'd come in early to check the footage and then decided to carefully edit this video. For Joq. He felt uneasy then. He knew Alison liked him, liked working for him. He also knew she didn't like what she'd seen in that kiss.

Joq watched them strip in the change room, still talking, laughing. He watched as they headed into the showers. He took a deep breath, hoping and not hoping she hadn't pulled up the footage from the showers.

She had. Finn was under his own shower, George next to him. Nothing in it. Good, Joq exhaled, still firmly in denial.

Finn was the one who moved. Joq didn't know why that surprised him, but it did. Finn turned off his shower and slid behind George under his spray. He wrapped his arms around George's waist, kissed his nape. George leaned back against him, craned his head back to say something. It was unbearably intimate. Joq wanted to turn it off. He'd seen this too, or a version of it; it still unsettled him, made him squirm.

George tugged Finn in front of him, pressed him against the tiles; and the expression on Finn's face was heated, turned on, but that's not all it was—it was adoring, it was naked and full of feeling. He was hiding nothing. George kissed him.

Finn's hand slipped down.

George stopped him. He said something against Finn's lips before reaching over to turn the tap off.

And, well, this was all pretty damning in the wrong hands. Joq couldn't believe George was being this fucking stupid, but as he watched them leave together—the footage jumping to them in the locker room, a careful distance apart as they got dressed—he realised the only really damning part was in the shower. And it was reasonable to assume George would think he was safe there—who wouldn't? It was a massive privacy violation to film in there and the only reason they had it was on an as-needs basis. No one was supposed to see this, even look for it. Alison had. And Joq knew why.

But as they were leaving, walking back up the tunnel and George stopped to turn the lights off, Joq wondered why she edited this part in when he saw it—George reached out and took Finn's hand. He slid their fingers together in a tight clasp. Their backs were to the tunnel, their bodies almost out of the shot, but there was enough light on the security footage for Joq to see it as George brought their joint hands up and kissed Finn's knuckles. They paused at the mouth of the tunnel, George's eyes looking up as Finn watched him back. George lowered their hands, tugged Finn in close, and their hands were still joined as they disappeared out of the shot.

Joq sank back in his chair. If he was waiting for a point for his denial to abate, this was it. He sat up and jumped back to the point where they were in the shower. He paused it. Minimised the video.

He had a plan now: he wasn't going to be made a fool of anymore. And while he was at it, he wasn't going to lose his boyfriend to some fucking sunshine rookie.

30

"**Y**OU SHOULD INVITE FINN for dinner again, before the Freo game," Joq said casually when he and George were watching TV later that week.

"Yeah?" George asked, turning to face him. "You think that's a good idea?"

"Why not? I mean, it was awkward, with the pool," he shrugged, feigning indifference. "Be nice to show him we're cool, you know."

"I dunno..."

"Come on, it's just fucking between you two, right?" Again, just be casual, Joq reminded himself, be cool.

George cleared his throat. "Yeah, course."

"And a bit of a crush," Joq really hammered up the easy-going enthusiasm on that line. It was not a fucking crush. No fucking way. The denial had fallen and he was mad. Really fucking mad.

George blushed.

"What about Thursday?"

George was shaking his head; Joq anticipated it. He knew George had a late meeting.

"Finn can come here from training, hang out for a bit while you're at the meeting," Joq leaned forward and picked up his beer. "I really want to let him know it's cool. I feel bad about, you know, giving him shit about PDAs in the pool."

George was nodding, his eyes on the TV, unseeing.

"Yeah, alright. I'll ask, but he might not be interested."

"Why?"

And here we go, Joq thought. This was coming out one way or another.

"Come on, Joq. He's a bit intimidated by you."

"Me?"

"Yeah, he's young, he's gonna get over this, you know, puppy love or whatever," George looked away, but he did not manage to hide how much it was cutting him up. Joq sympathised for a second. Then he wanted to pour his beer all over George's head.

He gripped the bottle tightly and replied. "Yeah, this'll probably help, if he sees it's cool. No hard feelings."

"I guess..."

"Cool."

"I'll ask."

"That's all I'm asking."

"Okay," George leaned forward and picked up the remote. "I can't watch anymore of this shit."

George loved this reality TV shit, so Joq knew he was looking for an out. He let him have it. He had a plan.

"Finn'll be here around seven," George said as he left for training Thursday morning.

"Cool," Joq smiled. "And you'll be done around eight?"

Joq did not expect Finn to still be here by then.

"Yeah," George said. He was zipping up his training bag, carefully not looking at Joq. It was clear he was not on board with this dinner, but Joq got the feeling he was trying to walk the middle ground—he seemed to believe he was a phase for Finn and was shoving his own feelings aside because of it and, for that reason, he was telling himself he was in a solid relationship with Joq.

Oh, Joq knew George loved him, but George was in love with Finn too. Joq knew that for a fact now, and he wasn't going to let it play out anymore.

"I'll keep him warm for you," Joq joked.

George went still.

"I'm joking, babe," Joq said, a bit pissed off.

"Yeah," George said, gruff. He didn't look at Joq as he said goodbye and left.

Ever late, Finn's "*It's me,*" came over the intercom at seven thirty.

Joq buzzed the gates open, clasped his tingling hands together. He wrung them out, turned the oven off, and went for the door.

"Finn, hey," Joq said as he opened it before Finn was up the steps.

Finn smiled up at him. He looked nervous, but relaxed too in the chill way that never seemed to leave him. His hair was mussed and longer than it had been at the start of the season. It looked almost blonder in parts, which was a mystery in the Victorian winter. His smile was close mouthed, eyes wary.

"Hey, Joq. Good to see you," he replied, ever polite.

"Come in, come in," Joq stepped aside.

He let the door swing shut with a click and watched Finn toe his shoes off. Finn was a large presence in the entrance of the house. All athletes had that impressive physical presence—the height, the muscles, the zero percent body fat—and Joq was used to it. But Finn's energy exuded a warm calmness Joq found irritating.

"Smells good," Finn said around his smile, head tilted so he was looking down at Joq to meet his eyes through the fall of his hair.

"Roast," Joq said. "Before we get to that, come with me. I want to show you something."

He moved past Finn and went for the stairs.

"Uhm, what?"

Joq glanced back. Finn was standing still, his socked feet on the carpet just inside the living room, his eyes uncertain around a nervous smile.

Joq laughed. "I'm not going to murder you, I just know George would want you to see this."

"See what?"

Goddamn kid was pretty fucking suspicious for all his hippy vibe.

"Memorabilia," Joq gave his best impression of being super impressed by elite athletes and their junk.

But Finn shook his head. "I don't feel comfortable going upstairs without George here."

And, wow. Joq had not expected this resistance, or directness. Kid was full of surprises. It made the mean part of Joq flare to life.

"Kid, I'm not going to jump you," Joq said, a hint of disgust in his voice.

Finn's eyebrows went up. "I think I can take you if you tried."

And, alright then. Kid was no pushover. Joq quickly changed tactics; it was an effort to stay nice, but he could do it.

He forced a laugh. "Take a seat," he waved at the living room. "I'll bring it down."

Finn nodded, like he'd won this round, and for a second he looked adorably young—like he was defending the honour of his relationship and fidelity to George and had made that clear. Which he had, Joq supposed as he jogged upstairs and went into his office, but it was the naivety of his youth showing if he thought he could win one battle and win the war.

Finn was perched on the edge of the couch, hands clasped, back erect, the perfect picture of discomfort when Joq came back down. His phone was on the coffee table in front of him.

Joq walked in with his laptop. Finn glanced at it, a hint of confusion on his face, words coming out of him like he'd been rehearsing them since Joq left him down here.

"George is on his way."

"You texted him?" Joq asked.

Finn nodded, eyes on the laptop as Joq put it on the coffee table and sat on the couch next to him. Finn shuffled over, creating more space between them.

"He's on his way home now," Finn said.

Joq wasn't sure if that was true—he wasn't due to finish until eight, and that's if they were on time; they usually weren't. Didn't matter—this would take around five minutes.

"Cool," Joq said and opened the laptop. "Check this out."

The video was already open, paused at the moment Finn's hand was turning his shower off. Joq hit play at the same time as Finn sucked in a breath.

"What's this?" fell faintly from his lips as his eyes widened.

Joq watched the video, but his attention was all on Finn next to him. Finn had gone completely still, a statue, even his breathing seemed to have stopped as he watched himself on screen slipping behind George, kissing his nape, on George turning him, on Finn's face before they kissed—turned on, vulnerable, in love—

"What is this?" Finn asked again.

"I think you know what this is," Joq said.

"Turn it off," Finn said on a desperate breath.

Joq looked at him. He'd expected shock, anger, even defiance. He hadn't expected pure terror. Joq didn't turn it off.

"What do you think will happen if this gets out?" Joq asked.

Finn sucked in a sharp breath. He looked at Joq and Joq saw him beginning to get it. Why Joq was showing him. What he wanted.

"You wouldn't do that to George," Finn said. He sounded sure, but one push and his certainty would crumble.

Joq closed the laptop. "Not to George, no."

Finn sighed, relieved.

"You would," Joq went on.

Finn looked confused.

"You think he'd stay with you after that got out? After you got him outed with something like that? Oh, he would at the start, but how do you think all that drama would work in your so called relationship? I know George, he's insanely private and this," Joq waved his hand at the laptop, "being out there? This is more than some rumour on a gay blog. He'd never get over it. It'd always be there. It'd destroy you from the start."

Finn had been breathing quietly as Joq spoke, his head shaking.

"But you wouldn't do that," he said again. "You wouldn't leak that."

"Tell you what, Finn," Joq leaned closer. Finn stilled. "I promise I'll destroy it if you leave my boyfriend alone. No more fucking, no more swimming and dates and whatever the fuck else you two are doing. And not a fucking word about this, you hear me?"

Finn was already nodding. Joq thought he'd put up more of a fight.

Joq bracketed his hand behind Finn's head on the couch and leaned in close; he could see Finn's pulse rabbiting in his throat, feel the fear coming off him.

"I thought you'd fight for him more than that," he whispered against Finn's ear.

"I'd never let anyone hurt him," Finn said, his voice shaking.

Joq laughed, low and mean; he tilted his head down so his breath ghosted over Finn's cheek.

"What the fuck?" came from behind them and Finn jerked back so quickly, he almost fell off the couch.

Joq leaned away at a more leisurely pace.

George was in the entryway, his fury writ large on his face, his body radiating with it. Joq felt Finn getting up behind him.

"It's not, George. It's not..." Finn's voice gave out. He sounded like he was about to cry.

"Finn?" George asked, a crack of sympathy in his anger.

Joq stood, placing his body between them. "Finn and I were just getting better acquainted. Right, Finn?" Joq looked over his shoulder and smiled at him, a clear warning.

All of Finn's composure was gone. He looked rattled to his core—his face was pale, his lips were parted, and his eyes had a sheen.

Joq thought about watching George fuck him, Finn's voice, '*Just yours*' and he narrowed his eyes.

He knew Finn got it then: one wrong fucking move, Joq said with that look. Finn swallowed. Joq waited, feeling almost giddy—he hadn't expected George to come home, but him finding them, assuming that, it was better than he could've imagined.

"I have to go," Finn said, his voice shaky, but there was a resolve there now too.

"Probably a good idea," Joq said. "Some other time maybe," he tacked on.

Finn flinched. He dropped his eyes and made for the hallway, giving Joq a wide berth.

"Hang on," George said. He was still angry, but Joq saw he was confused too. "Finn, what's going on?"

Finn was shaking his head and reaching for his shoes, his face covered by his hair.

"Let him go, babe," Joq said. "We didn't think you'd be back so soon."

He watched that land: Finn sucked in a breath, but kept his head down, fumbled with his shoes. George looked like he'd been punched in the face.

"No," he said, turning to Finn. "No, Finn. What's he...what... "

But Finn was up, his head shaking, his breathing rough and wet. He was out the door before George could move.

"What the fuck was that?" George asked and turned to Joq.

Joq shrugged. "Fucking around? I dunno, it just kinda happened. Or started to."

"No," George said again, his head shaking. Joq couldn't quite believe this had turned out so well. He'd had no intention of trying to hook up with Finn, of even making it look like that was about to happen; but it was a perfect final nail in the coffin.

"He wouldn't..." George said like he was shell-shocked.

Joq picked up his laptop. "I'm sorry," he said as somberly as he could. "He did."

"Did you... What did you—

"Tread carefully, George," Joq said, his tone metal. "You've known me a long time. You think I go around hitting on kids who don't want it?"

And Joq knew he had him then. He watched the gears turn. Because Joq was right. He'd never do that—and up until Finnegan Flynn walked into his life, he never thought he'd do what he'd just done either. He waited to feel bad about it, but all he felt in that moment was self-righteous victory.

"You're right, I'm sorry," George dropped his head.

Joq exhaled. He went by him and headed for the stairs.

"Dinner's ready," he said and went for his office.

He was removing the USB stick, tucking it into his bag when he heard George's car starting. He peered out the window in time to see him gunning it out the gates and just miss scratching his car as he barely waited for the gap.

George came back a couple of hours later. Joq found him in the kitchen. He was bracing his hands on the bench, shoulders hunched with his head hanging between them.

"It's over," he said before Joq could speak.

"What happened?" Joq asked, faux-sympathetically.

George shook his head. "He wouldn't let me in."

Joq sighed. He didn't know what to say. How did one sympathise when their boyfriend had an emotional affair on them? All he felt was anger, which was finally giving way to some relief.

"Sorry," he settled on, a moment too late.

George dragged in a deep breath. "No, I'm sorry," he looked up and out at the pool, exhaled roughly. "It was more than fucking. For me. It was unfair to you."

Joq could see George's eyes shining from the light from the microwave and he knew the sentiment was sincere. He thought that would make him feel better. He'd known it was more than fucking, of course he had, he hadn't turned into a villain from some psychopath movie over nothing. But the confirmation broke his heart just a little bit more.

"It's okay," he managed. "It's over now."

"It is," George said firmly. He stood tall and carefully didn't touch Joq as he went for the fridge, grabbed a beer, then headed outside.

Joq stood in the darkness of the kitchen and watched George sit in the cabana, drink his beer, eyes on the pool, every inch of him a picture of defeat.

31

H IS PHONE WAS PINGING. Joq groaned and rolled over, stretched his arm out. The bed was empty. Cold. His phone pinged again. And again. He rolled back and slapped his hand on the bedside table until he found it and brought it into his line of sight.

News notifications. A few texts. Finn's name and season over?

Joq sat up and clicked on the top story.

Finnegan Flynn out for the rest of the season for mental health reasons.

Joq sucked in a breath and read the story. It was short and to the point: Finn was out, some bullshit about the side-effects of his concussion leaving a lingering depression and he wouldn't finish the season.

His phone pinged with a new notification.

Breaking: Finnegan Flynn traded.

No way, no team would trade a player over this, it'd be public relations suicide—

Then he read the article: Trade was requested. Sydney. Closer to home. To family and friends with his current difficulties.

Joq flung the covers off and went downstairs. George was pulling his shoes on.

"Did he tell you?" Joq asked.

"He won't take my calls," George replied and slammed out the door.

Well, fuck.

Joq watched the news and Talking Heads all day with a mix of horror and fascination. There was a lot of quiet speculation, but everyone carefully talked around it. No one was going to call bullshit on a player for citing mental health problems, even if it seemed a lot of them wanted to call the kid a pussy who couldn't handle being that far away from home. Combine this drama with his late entry to the league because of a slow recovery from injury and Joq could see the presenters were trying very hard not to call him weak.

It was late when George came back.

Joq stood from the couch. "Did you speak to him?"

George shook his head. "He's gone."

"Whaddya mean he's gone?"

"He left last night," George was toeing his shoes off, looking anywhere but at Joq. "Flew home."

"Fuck," Joq breathed out.

George didn't reply. He kept his face averted and went upstairs. Joq heard the shower turn on. He sat back down and changed the channel. It was all anyone was talking about, so he switched to streaming and waited for George to come back down.

Eventually, Joq had to concede he wasn't coming back, and he turned everything off and headed to bed.

George was there, in the dark, and very awake.

Joq's eyes adjusted as he got in and saw George's fixed on the ceiling.

"Freo tomorrow," he said.

"Yep," George replied and rolled over, giving Joq his back.

32

THE FREO GAME WAS an embarrassing thrashing. Joq wanted to be able to tease George about it—see, I told you, play them in the dry and they'll thump you—but they were absolutely not in that place.

And besides, the crushing defeat Freo handed them was as much on them losing as it was on Freo playing a blinder of a game. Jack Reaver was in form, and he and Hiller made highlight-reel play after play—getting it clean off the centre bounce, Hiller ran like he had his own personal wind at his back, made a no-look kick right into Jack's chest, then kick, goal. Variation after variation between them; it was beautiful football. Or, it would've been, if Joq could get past the hollowness of his own team, the hole of defeat radiating from them from the first centre bounce.

It wasn't just the loss of their star player. Joq knew they'd be calling bullshit on Finn's reason. On the fact he just fled. Requested a trade. One day he's messing around in the locker room and laughing and the next, he's what, depressed and can't play? Bullshit.

Joq wanted to feel bad about the whole thing, and he almost did, but when he got to work and met Alison's knowing look, he felt guilty, yes, but he'd get over it. What else was he supposed to do?

After the game, he went down to the tunnel to catch up with Jack. He didn't expect to see George any time soon; his stormy expression throughout the game actually made him hope he wouldn't. Maybe Jack would be interested in grabbing a drink.

"Joq," Jack smiled big and warm when he emerged from the visitor's locker room. He looked great in his suit, his easy manner a breath of fresh air over Joq's current reality.

"Hey, super star," Joq smiled at him.

"Ah, shut it," Jack smiled and came in for a hug. "How's it goin'? Sorry about the game," he made a genuine face of displeasure because if anyone was genuinely sorry to destroy the team you support even though it meant he'd just won, it was Jack.

"Nah, all good. You're looking well," Joq appraised him. He was. He'd filled out more since he left, was more of a man than the boy Joq had known.

"You too," Jack nudged him, hoisted his duffel up his shoulder. "George good?"

"Yeah, he's alright."

"Cool, cool, it's just. I know he was pissed about the trade, but I thought that was all done," Jack looked away as he spoke, shook his head.

"It is? I mean, yeah, he's always gonna carry a grudge about it, but it's not like he doesn't still love you, man."

Jack looked at him. "He ignored me when I said hello, wouldn't even look at me."

Oh. Joq had been hoping to avoid mentioning Finn.

"Yeah, think with this new trade..."

"Oh, yeah, shit," Jack got real animated. "What the fuck happened? I know Finn, that's not like him."

"You know Finn?"

"Yeah, course—

"Ah, here he is!" Sean Hiller shouted as he came out of the locker room, the door clanging shut behind him. Jack cut off at the sound of his voice, his whole body tensing.

Hiller came up beside him. His smile was huge, and a little bit mean. He glanced at Joq and extended his hand and his face transformed into the laconic, easy smile everyone knew well.

"Sean Hiller," he said. Joq shook his hand.

"Joaquin Nord," he replied and couldn't help returning the smile. Hiller's charm was infectious, more so in person. He was also one of the greatest players in the game today. Not one of the greatest Indigenous players, one of the greatest, period, and he wore that position with enviable ease.

He turned back to Jack, his smile turning indulgent. "Jack, Jack, Jackie, what's the aim of the game, eh? Kick through the middle, the middle."

Joq knew he was referring to the couple of points Jack had kicked from dead in front. Not that they'd mattered.

"Jesus, Hiller. Save it for video review," Jack sounded tired.

Hiller clapped him on the back and Joq watched Jack shudder at the touch; his eyes slipped closed, his body went rigid. Hiller squeezed.

"Alright, we'll watch it in slow mo., eh?" he laughed, squeezed again. "Are you coming to the bus or you gonna stay here tonight?"

"I'll be there in a sec," Jack replied, voice soft.

Hiller let go, his hand dragging down Jack's back, his eyes on him, something inexplicably angry in his look.

But then he was turning to Joq like that hadn't happened at all, all smiles. "Nice to meet you."

And he was gone.

"What was that all about?"

"Don't ask," Jack rubbed his face. "I better go, but can you tell George I said hi? I don't want bad blood between us."

"Course, yeah, but I wouldn't worry about it. You guys are cool."

"Are you sure because—

"Jack, bus is leaving," one of the trainers said as he walked past.

"Yep," Jack hoisted his bag higher. "Come see me in Perth sometime."

Joq snorted. "Okay, if I ever find myself in Perth..."

Jack laughed, leaned in to hug him again, slapped him on the back and jogged up the tunnel, his "Later, Joq," carrying down the concrete walls.

Joq pulled out his phone and texted the uni friend group chat. He headed back up to the room, listened to his phone ping. Surely one of them would want to go out, save Joq from having to go home.

It was the early hours of the morning when he stumbled in after bar-hopping his way through Fitzroy. He expected George to be asleep. He was surprised to see him sitting out by the pool, still in his suit and big coat, empty beer bottles near his socked feet as he stared at the water, turning his phone over in his hands.

Joq got butterflies; George had waited up for him.

"Hey," he said, slightly slurred as he went outside.

George startled, his eyes bleary. "Oh, Joq. Hey."

"Havin' a party?" Joq nodded at the bottles. He wanted to go over and sit next to him, but something was telling him through the alcohol he shouldn't.

George ignored the remark.

"You went out?" he asked like he didn't really care.

"Obviously," Joq said. Getting rid of Finn was supposed to make it all better, but it felt all wrong. Give it time, he told himself. It'll right itself.

"Sorry," George shook his head and went back to turning his phone in his hands.

"You comin' to bed?"

George rubbed his eyes, shook his head.

"Look," Joq said, the alcohol making him brave. "I know Finn leaving sucks, but you'll rebuild. It'll be fine, maybe not this year, but you're a rookie too, you know? Just get through the season."

George's shoulders started to shake. Joq squinted, felt terrible. Then he realised George was laughing.

"What's so funny?"

"Nothin', sorry," George met his eyes across the pool. "Nothin'."

Joq smiled. "No, tell me."

George smiled the unhappiest smile Joq had ever seen. "You think I give a shit about the season?"

"Well, yeah..."

"Look," George met his eyes. "I know this is not fair to you, I know that. But I'm gonna need some time, okay? It wasn't... nothing."

Joq looked away, at the manicured gardens around the pool, the palm trees swaying in the light breeze, their summery feel at odds with the winter chill around them.

"I didn't mean for this to happen," George went on, his own tongue clearly loosened by the booze. Joq wanted to tell him to shut up. "And I know it's not fair to you," he rambled on again. "So, if you want out, I get it."

And that sobered Joq right up. "What're you saying? You want to break up?"

George shook his head. "No, but I'm saying I get it if you do 'cos I'm asking for some time to, you know," he looked at his phone, "get over him."

Joq's stomach dropped out. The world stopped spinning for a moment. He watched George staring at his phone. His shoulders were hunched, and his heartbreak was evident in every line of his body.

"Are you still speaking to him?" Joq asked, eyes on the phone.

George jerked his head. "He blocked me."

And well, it wasn't as good as George initiating no contact, but it was better than nothing.

"Just," Joq sighed. "Let's talk after the season ends."

"Okay," George was nodding. "I've moved into the spare room, so, you can have some space while I..."

Joq didn't know what to say, and George didn't go on. So, he said nothing and went back inside.

33

BEFORE FINN LEFT, THE team had been solid finals contenders. Not top four, but they'd been pencilled in to make the eight. Now, Joq watched as they battled it out in a game that meant the difference between bottom of the eight or season over.

In the end, it was barely a contest. They were out, season done. They still had games to play, but they were out.

Things at home were polite, friendly, a couple of housemates careful not to say the wrong thing. Joq hated it.

But once the final game was done, it was George who said they should get away, maybe Thailand.

Joq was already looking at flights before George had finished speaking.

And then a social media storm erupted with one photo and everything in Joq's careful plan to rebuild his relationship screeched to a halt.

A funny little voice above the noise and disbelief in his brain thought, *It's actually a good picture.*

It was Finn, no mistake, his face turned to the camera, his lips parted, hair mussed, eyes bleary with booze, a big burly guy pressing him up against a wall, lips fused to the side of his neck, their bodies pressed tightly together. The photo was tagged at a gay club in Sydney, the caption leaving no room for tossing this out as a one-off, drunken kiss: *and this was before he got railed in the bathroom...*

The media went ballistic, the voices shouting about outing someone without their consent drowning out the other voices that sounded self-satisfied in finally questioning the "depression" line. The picture was taken down, but it was too late. It was screenshotted. It was everywhere.

Joq clicked to a video of Finn trying to leave his house in Byron, his mother and his sister with him, the sister telling the reporters to "Fuck off!" while Finn looked stoic yet terrified in the middle of their huddle.

He heard George make a guttural sound behind him. Joq slammed his laptop shut. He looked up. George was breathing loudly, and he seemed angry, yes, but upset too.

"He'll—"

"Don't," George said and went for the door, grabbed his coat, keys, pulled on his boots and left.

When George still wasn't back the next morning, it finally dawned on Joq he'd gone to see Finn. To console him.

Joq didn't know how to feel about that. Pissed off, certainly, that old self-righteous anger raising its head again. It was almost becoming a comfort.

It was a feeling that deflated suddenly and thoroughly when he finally got a text from George twenty-four hours after he'd walked out the door.

I know what you did.

Joq felt all the life drain out of him. He wished he'd never done it. He wanted to take it back. He had no idea how he'd fix this. He typed and erased several messages. By the time he finally sent one line, *I can explain*, the message bounced. Blocked.

And it was not George he spoke to about where they went next, it was George's lawyer.

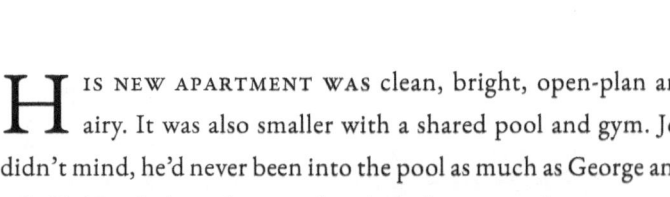

His new apartment was clean, bright, open-plan and airy. It was also smaller with a shared pool and gym. Joq didn't mind, he'd never been into the pool as much as George and, as he'd thought bitterly since the whole thing went down, as much as George and Finn together. He heard through the grapevine George had sold the place, where he lived now a mystery. Where he was now also a mystery. He hadn't been in the stadium: "on leave" the only explanation that'd been given.

Joq had a pretty good idea that leave was happening in Byron Bay. He tried not to think about it. He felt like shit about what he'd done, and that feeling had been cemented when George's lawyer presented him with a settlement document—effectively ending their de-facto relationship with a pay out and a request to be out of the place by the end of the week. Joq still had the cheque; he didn't think he'd cash it, the whole thing felt too shitty.

So, he was surprised when he got a message from a private number to meet up at a dive bar in St Kilda signed off, *Creed*.

Joq had to snort. Really? The unceremonious lawyer, paperwork, removal truck at ass o'clock exactly seven days after George left didn't tip him off there was nothing but frosty animosity between them from now on? Oh, yes, signing off Creed would do it.

He wasn't going to go. What was there to say?

Well, actually, he thought the day after receiving the message, and the day before they were set to meet, there was a lot to fucking say. He woke up pissed off and replied: *See you then*. He stopped himself from writing *Nord* in a fit of pettiness.

The bar was dark when he walked in, the early afternoon sunshine muted through the cracked blinds. There were a few people on one side, in shadows, a lady playing a poky near them, the bar on the far side empty. Joq sat on a bar stool on the pty side.

"What can I get ya?"

"Schooner of whatever pale you've got on tap," Joq said and put his wallet on the bar.

The guy brought his drink. Joq tapped his card. He took a sip and ignored the sound of the door opening, the jangle of the blinds clapping against the glass.

George cleared his throat. Joq looked up. He was tanner, his hair even longer, and underneath the carefully concealed fury radiating off him, he looked better and more relaxed than he had in a long time. Joq guessed marathon fucking a twenty-year-old would do that.

"Have a seat," Joq said.

"This won't take long," George replied.

Joq turned to face him.

"What can I get ya?" the bartender asked.

"Nothin'," George shot him a smile. "Thanks."

The bartender wandered off, his wide eyes saying he knew exactly who he'd just spoken to. George waited until he was on the other side of the bar before he spoke again.

"I wanted to say this in person so you didn't have any evidence."

Joq scoffed. "Odd to come to a bar to do it if you're not gonna have a drink."

"I wanted to make it public so I couldn't punch you in the fucking face."

"That's rich," Joq sneered, all his guilt replaced with anger. "Twelve fucking years, George."

"You think twelve years gave you the right to blackmail him? You think you can justify that?" he was keeping his voice low, but he was seething.

Joq took a long drink of his beer. His voice was calm when he spoke.

"Yeah, and you know what else I think? I've still got that footage, so I'd think long and hard about what it is you've come here to say."

George laughed, his eyes dancing when they met Joq's. "I can't believe I never saw it before. He said, but I never saw it."

"What?" Joq feigned boredom, acted like he didn't care about what that little shit had said.

"You never loved me," George said. He said it like it was a relief to get it out there.

"What the fuck—

"You didn't. Oh, you were fond of me, we had some good times. But it wasn't love."

"Oh, yeah? You a fucking expert now?"

George sobered. "Yeah, I am actually. The real thing? You'd never do that to the real thing, you'd let th go."

And that was a low fucking blow. It could only be met with a lower blow.

"Still got that footage, George," he drained his drink and held up a finger to the bartender.

He felt George breathing next to him, felt him smiling. George waited until the bartender had left again, his effusive, "Sure I can't get you something?" met with George's blinding grin, "I'm good."

"That's what I came to talk to you about," George said around his smile.

"Oh yeah?" Joq didn't like that smile.

"Release it. Sell it. Do whatever the fuck you want with it," he leaned down and spoke against Joq's ear, "' when I marry him next month, I want everyone to see what I'm getting. I want the whole world to replace the image of the other piece of shit you drove him to with the image of me."

He leaned back.

Joq was speechless.

George winked. "I wouldn't mind seeing it myself, Finn said it was pretty fucking hot."

"Yeah, after he cried about it," Joq spat.

George's candour evaporated and he was furious again. "I'd think very carefully about what you say about him, Joaquin. I promised him I wouldn't hit you, but I think he'd understand."

Joq took a long drink. "Good to see you got another guy to do your thinking for you."

George smiled again. "Release it," he repeated and turned to walk out.

"Oh, and Joq?"

Joq looked over.

"Speak to him again and I'll hit you with a lawsuit for extortion so fast, you'll wonder what the fuck hit you."

And with that, he left, the door clanging quietly behind him.

"Shit, that was George Creed," the bartender said as he came back over.

"Yep," Joq drained his beer, nodded when the bartender picked up a glass for another.

The door clanged open and a couple of guys in high vis came in.

"Guess who we just saw walking down the street?" one of them asked as he took a seat.

"George Creed?" the bartender replied, his smile indulgent.

"And Finnegan Flynn," the other one said. "Man, I ain't gay, but I would for him, fuck."

Joq laughed, what else could he do?

Epilogue

It was a year later when Joq finally booked those plane tickets to Thailand. He had a new boyfriend, very new, only just at the stage where they'd shifted from fucking to dating to Chris asking seriously and nervously if they could be exclusive.

"Not open?"

"Definitely not," Chris had replied, affronted as they had the conversation in a coffee shop, Chris anxiously stirring his coffee until that moment. "I don't want to share you."

And, well, sue him, that line made Joq preen, made him think maybe he'd get his forever love too.

He'd suggested Koh Samui for a summer break, and Chris had booked a month off from his brokerage firm the next day, booked them first class seats and sent Joq a link to a resort. Joq knew the place, of course; it was the best, with exclusive bungalows and private beaches. He couldn't see any reason to say no.

He'd made his peace with George and Finn. Well, he felt like he had.

He hadn't released the footage.

For one thing, if that got out, there'd be a lot of questions about how someone got access. Worse, if he didn't own it, they'd grill his team. Ask for a scapegoat. He'd never do that to them.

And for another thing, he felt the never-ending news coverage, social media trending, and gossip rag coverage of the wedding was sufficient, thanks.

The image of George's arms holding Finn tight against him, Finn's hands bunched in the back of George's white shirt, their bodies fused together while they shared a kiss way too passionate for a bloody wedding ceremony was enough.

It was about a month after the wedding when he felt like he couldn't escape the photos and clips—George and Finn barefoot on the beach in matching loose white pants and shirts, tanned and smiling at one another; champagne glasses clinking with eyes only for the other in a marquee filled with fairy lights and flowers; their first dance and George's lips in Finn's hair, whispering something as Finn smiled a private smile—when Joq got really drunk, cried a little, and did something with the footage.

He woke up the next day, saw the notification on his phone informing him his parcel was on its way to the PO Box registered on Finn's social media accounts, and he felt, not better, but relieved.

He received a thank you note weeks later, embossed in wedding calligraphy; it was an actual thank you note from their wedding, signed, *Finn & George*.

Joq tossed it in the bin. He tried not to think about how he was going to face George at work that season.

George took care of that though. Got himself a trade to Sydney, assistant coach for the other Sydney side, and Joq had to put up with another news cycle obsessed with the married rivals. But the season passed with nothing in it, and Joq had to concede Finn didn't deal with as much homophobia as people expected—having George watch all of his games that didn't conflict with his own schedule from a corporate box looking like he'd serial kill everyone who looked at Finn the wrong way probably helped.

It was finals when he met Chris. It was offseason when they went exclusive. And as Joq got out of their transfer limousine and stepped into the humid Thai sunshine, he felt good.

"I'll check us in," Chris said as he came up beside Joq, squeezed his hip. "Go have a drink."

Joq smiled up at him. "See you at the pool bar."

He made his way through the plant-filled lobby, gazed at the palms and the beach beyond, felt the warm breeze like a welcome hit of calm. He was making his way outside to the patio, heading for the bar when he saw him.

His eyes landed on the gold wedding band like it was a magnet. Finn was walking his way, dressed casually in shorts and a nice button up, his hair long, skin tanned, body bigger. He saw Joq a moment after Joq saw him, and he started, eyes widening in surprise. Joq thought he'd look away, walk on. He didn't; he smiled, walked right up to him.

"Joq, hey," he said as he stopped a careful distance away.

"Finn," Joq nodded.

"How's it going?" Finn asked, calm and happy.

"I'm not supposed to talk to you," Joq replied and cringed inwardly.

But Finn laughed. "It's in the past, eh," he brought his hand up, wiggled his fingers so his wedding band was on display. "You staying here?"

"Yep, Chris, my boyfriend, is checking us in," he said and felt that old surreal feeling come back. Finn had that effect on him.

Finn nodded affably though, still smiling, glanced towards the lobby. "George is checking us out. Probably for the best," he looked back at Joq and quirked his lips.

Joq was relieved. He tried to return the smile.

"Well, I better," Finn waved a hand. "Nice seeing you."

And then Joq felt angry; Finn was so chill, it was like he'd forgotten about the part he played in the whole mess.

"I can't say the same," he said and watched the smile slip from Finn's face. "Yeah, what I did was shitty and I'm sorry, I really am. But you stole my boyfriend and no one seems to care about that part."

Finn laughed, high and light, his smile back in full force. He met Joq's gaze head on, that same defiance Joq remembered well glinting in his eyes. "Oh, Joq. You still believe that?"

"I know that."

"How could I steal something that was already mine?"

Joq frowned at the illogic of that statement.

"Twelve years, me and George—

"He was never yours," Finn cut him off. "He was always mine, you were just keeping him company until I arrived."

Joq started to shake his head. Finn smiled at him, there was nothing mean in it, just a genuine, radiant smile.

"Well, keep telling yourself that if it makes you feel better," Joq said and went to walk to the bar.

"I don't have to," Finn said. Joq turned to look at him. He was smiling, confident and beautiful. "He does."

Joq felt that like a slap. Even after everything, he was surprised it could hurt.

"Later, Joq," Finn said and headed into the lobby.

Joq watched as he slipped up beside George at the counter, George's arm going around him like it was natural, turning to press a kiss to Finn's lips like he did it all the time, there in a public lobby with tourists and phone cameras and the possibility for the world to see.

"You haven't had a drink yet?" Chris asked as he walked up.

Joq startled, tore his eyes away.

"Not yet," Joq smiled.

"Wanna go to the bungalow then? I've ordered champagne."

And yeah, Joq really did. He spared another glance at George and Finn, expected them to be looking his way, for Finn to have said something. They weren't. George was looking at Finn, his hand running up and down his back, while Finn laughed and gave him a playful shove, the two of them firmly entrenched in their own world, the same way they'd been since the first time Joq saw them on TV, in the tunnel, on the surveillance tape; eyes always and only for each other.

Acknowledgments

My biggest thanks to Ana: for the idea, for workshopping it with me, for beta reading, and for doing the final read through. Her beta feedback nuanced parts of this and added some much needed depth—this is a better story thanks to her contributions. Thanks as well to KP for the thoughtful and honest remarks: 'Some people will hate this one'(!). And DF for cross-checking my AFL knowledge; shout out as well to my middle brother on this front for creating Finn's backstory. As always, thank you to my editor—the mighty Kath!—for getting this done in the midst of a personal crisis. And thank you to Cate Ashwood for the wonderful cover. Finally, thank you to my mailing list! Your thoughts and input give me life.

About Author

Sasha Avice is the author of seven novels (and counting!) and one PhD (which is enough). She lives with a changing cast of birds and a dog. When she's not writing or teaching, she's fostering birds. She loves hearing from readers! Email direct at sasha@sashaavice.com or join her mailing list at sashaavice.com for fortnightly updates.

Also By

Because He's My Guy

A Contested Possession Novel

**He's been in an open relationship for twelve years
He's never touched another guy...
Until him.**

George Creed will soon debut as the youngest coach in Australian
Football history.
He's excited, he's nervous.
He's more obsessed with meeting his new rookie.

Finnegan Flynn is finally joining the team after being sidelined with injury for two seasons. As the number one draft pick, he's got a lot to prove.

He's more obsessed with meeting his new coach—his footy idol and teenage crush.

When George invites Finn over for dinner, Finn suspects they're about to take their budding attraction to the next level. Until he meets George's boyfriend, Joaquin.

Finn is crushed, but George explains he's in an open relationship. Except George doesn't do open, he's a one man kind of guy.

Finn is utterly confused: if George doesn't do open, why tell him?

Because George isn't open, until he meets Finn.

But if George is a one man kind of guy, then whose guy is he?

The second novel in the *Contested Possession* series, *Because He's My Guy* is *His Boyfriend's Rookie* according to George and Finn. Each novel stands alone.

You Could Do Better
A Contested Possession Novel

"You don't look at me like a hook-up."
"How do I look at you?"
"I don't know. But it's not like that."

Chris McLachlan can't stop thinking about the cool guy he met at a rooftop bar. So when he crashes into him at his favourite coffee shop a year later, he asks him out immediately. He's bewildered when he gets turned down cold—he's a decent looking billionaire, is this guy for real? Sure, Chris has a sexual problem, but this guy doesn't know that.

After his messy break-up, Joaquin Nord never wants to date again. Riddled with feelings of betrayal, shame and depression, he's content to keep to himself and avoid all things George and Finn—his ex and the rookie he married a month after they broke up—for the rest of his life. He's definitely not going to date the weird guy who keeps rocking up at his coffee place.

But when Joq is subjected to yet another installment of the Gay Football Soap Opera that is George and Finn in the media, he decides to give Chris a shot. Losing himself in a hot one night stand is just the ticket he needs to move on.

But from the first night, it feels like more than a hook-up. For Chris, it's the first time he's slept with someone he wants to see again. For Joq, it's far too intimate.

Joq won't do another relationship. And Chris can't because he's sexually dysfunctional. It makes no sense for them to keep hooking up.

And yet, they do, repeatedly, both of them waiting for the other shoe to drop...

Until Joq realises he can't do better, but can Chris?

Perimeter

"Out here on the perimeter, we ain't interested in love... but goddamn if it don't keep on finding us."

Set in Western Australia at the turn of the millennium, each book is a standalone featuring guys who don't want love, don't seek it.

They drift, they work... and then some guy turns up and the dull isolation goes bright, blinds them like a splinter of sun caught in the eyes.

Available Now in the *Perimeter* Series:

Fox

You Were My Ride Or Die

The Cook

After the Show

This Ain't No Gay Romance